"You Want M...
Kan...

"Just once." She tapped her forefinger on her lips. "Right here. Just so I can see ..." She didn't think she had to tell him exactly what she wanted to *see*.

"Okay," he said doubtfully. "But this doesn't mean anything."

The moment his mouth closed over hers, she felt the surge of power, the quickening of her pulse, the sense of thrill, and she clung to him, insisting on more. Fire spread down her neck and into her chest. Another moment...just another moment...

Drawing back, he stared at her. She reached out and touched the palm of her hand to his cheek.

"Thank you..." she said breathlessly.

Dear Reader,

This month it seems like everyone's in romantic trouble. We have runaway brides and jilted grooms…They've been left at the altar and wonder if they'll *ever* find true love with the right person.

Of course they do, and we get to find out how, as we read Silhouette Desire's delightful month of "Jilted!" heroes and heroines.

And what better way to start this special month than with *The Accidental Bridegroom*, a *Man of the Month* from one of your favourites, Ann Major? We're sure you'll enjoy this passionate story of seduction and supposed betrayal as much as we did.

And look for five more fabulous books by some of your most beloved writers: Dixie Browning, Cait London, Raye Morgan, Jennifer Greene and Cathie Linz. Yes, their characters might have been left at the altar…but they don't stay single for long!

So don't pick and choose—read about them all! We loved these stories, and are sure you will, too.

Jane Nicholls
Silhouette Books
PO Box 236
Thornton Road
Croydon
Surrey
CR9 3RU

Sorry, the Bride Has Escaped

RAYE MORGAN

SILHOUETTE
Desire

*First published in Great Britain in 1995
by Silhouette Books, Eton House, 18-24 Paradise Road,
Richmond, Surrey TW9 1SR*

© Helen Conrad 1994

*Silhouette, Silhouette Desire and Colophon are
Trade Marks of Harlequin Enterprises B.V.*

ISBN 0 373 59616 2

22-9504

Made and printed in Great Britain

RAYE MORGAN

favours settings in the West, which is where she has spent most of her life. She admits to a penchant for Western heroes, believing that whether he's a rugged outdoorsman or a smooth city sophisticate, he tends to have a streak of wildness that the romantic heroine can't resist taming. She's been married to one of those Western men for twenty years and is busy raising four more in her Southern California home.

Other Silhouette Books by Raye Morgan

Silhouette Desire

One

Housebreaking. Just one more talent to add to her list.

Ashley laughed aloud, then clamped a hand over her mouth and looked around a little wildly. The sound of her own voice was eerie in the dark room.

Not that anyone was likely to hear her. The nearest neighbors were beyond a huge stand of banyan trees, and from what she'd seen in a week of casing the joint, no one was living in the house itself. Which was very convenient, since her only alternative would be to go stay in a cave for a week. And that didn't seem especially appealing.

"I'm afraid that would be cold," she murmured to herself as she made her way through the house. "And rather damp."

Speaking of cold and damp, her wedding dress was beginning to feel exactly that. She'd had to make a run for it, through wet grass and the edges of the bay, then she'd ripped out the hem climbing into this little refuge through the back window. It was definitely time for a change of clothing.

There wasn't a lot of choice. She returned to the bedroom she'd entered through and looked around.

"I just need to borrow a few things," she whispered to the absent landlord as she puttered through his chest of drawers. "I'll bring everything back clean and pressed. I promise."

Unfortunately, it seemed the dear gentleman was unmarried. Everything she found was made for a male. "Yuppie male," she muttered, looking through the polo shirts and camp shorts, searching in vain for jeans and a raggedy T-shirt.

Finally she settled for a long-sleeved dress shirt that would reach her knees, and as she pulled down the wedding dress, it hit the ground with a thunk.

Sighing with relief, she slipped into the white shirt and turned to explore the house. A bright flash of light and a sudden rumble stopped her in her tracks. Lightning. The storm that had been threatening was finally here. Pulling her arms in tightly, she shivered.

"Good thing I'm not superstitious," she reminded herself doubtfully. "Otherwise, I would take this as a bad sign."

Bad sign—good grief! As if she hadn't had enough of those today. She should be immune to bad luck by now, she'd had plenty of inoculations. A slightly hysterical bubble of laughter threatened again, but she held it back and returned to the business of exploring her hideout.

The investigation didn't take very long. Even in the gathering gloom, it only took a few minutes to see what there was to see. It was a typical beach house, open and airy, with two bedrooms in the back and a living room that opened onto a lanai overlooking the bay. Although it was only about half a mile from the church where people were probably still milling, waiting for her to show up and marry Wesley, she was sure no one would find her here. No one would even think to look in this direction.

Did she dare turn on a light? It was getting very dark, making her nervous. She didn't want a neighbor to notice. Still, she couldn't just sit in the middle of the floor and wait for morning. Tentatively, she turned on the light in the back hallway and immediately felt better.

Relief lasted only seconds though. Another bright flash of lightning brought a clap of thunder, and the light was gone just as suddenly as it had appeared. The electricity had obviously been knocked out by the storm.

Ashley's moan of agony was cut short. Lights flashed outside again, but this time it wasn't nature. A car was pulling up in the driveway.

"No," she said out loud, hardly believing her eyes. It couldn't be. She'd looked this place over all week during her many long, lonely walks along the beach. She was sure no one was staying here. How could it be possible that the owner would return on the very night she needed it so badly?

A shadow passed the front window and a key was rattling in the door. There was no time to argue with fate. Someone was definitely coming in to join her.

Spinning, she made a run for the back of the house, slipping into one of the bedrooms, heading for the closet. She flung herself in among the hanging clothes and pulled the sliding door shut behind her, then leaned against the wall, heart thumping, peering out the crack she'd left herself.

It was a man. Ashley could tell by his heavy footsteps and by the muttered curse he uttered when he tried the lights and found them dead. She heard a suitcase hit the floor, then his footsteps going off toward the kitchen area.

Should she make a run for it? She hesitated, not sure what to do. She couldn't stay here. She didn't relish being found out and spending what should have been her wedding night in the local jail.

But going outside in a man's shirt with little else under it, and running around looking for shelter from the pouring rain didn't have much appeal, either. What the heck was she going to do now?

She should have had a better plan from the beginning. That was the story of her life. No plan. Sometimes she feared she really was as reckless as people said. Why did she do these things?

Never mind. The point now was, what was she going to do about the situation? Cautiously, she began to ease the sliding door open, but a flickering light coming from the hallway stopped her short. He'd found a candle, and he was coming her way.

Maybe if she held her breath...maybe if she stayed very still.... But her gaze fell on the wedding dress lying in a heap in the middle of the floor, and she froze. There was no way the man could ignore that. He was sure to wonder.

"What the hell ... ?"

He'd seen it. Ashley drew back and bit her lip, trying not to breathe or even think. He stared down at the wedding dress for a long moment, then his gaze rose and he saw the open window, the window she'd climbed in through. Cursing under his breath, he went toward it, holding the candle high.

Ashley took advantage of her opportunity, sliding the closet door carefully open and slipping out. No more hesitating; she had to get out of there, fast. She would be stealing his shirt, she thought to herself, but, what the heck? He could have the wedding dress in exchange.

She reached the front door in record time, running as though the hounds of hell were nipping at her heels. Her fingers wrapped around the knob but as she turned it nothing happened. The handle spun loosely, not connecting with the lock, and the door wouldn't budge.

Whirling around, she flattened herself against the door and scanned the dark room, her breath coming ragged in her throat. He was still in the bedroom. Her only hope was the back door, through the kitchen. She took off again, praying he wouldn't come into the hallway as she slipped past the bedroom door.

Kam Caine was having a very bad day. Hell, it had been a bad month. A bad year. And only a so-so lifetime. At least, that was the way he felt about it at the moment. He was definitely stressed out, and he'd come out to his beach house for a long weekend for some rest and relaxation, hoping to get his equilibrium back—along with his smile.

What he needed was about forty-eight hours of deep sleep and to wake up for a swim in the bay and a cool drink in the sand. What he did not need was a raging tropical storm or an intruder in his house.

The open window was a bad sign. Whoever it was who'd left that pile of rags on the floor was probably still in the house.

He turned, frowning. He thought he'd heard something, but the clatter of the rain on his roof made it hard to distinguish lesser sounds. Still, he had a feeling....

He went back to the bundle on the floor, holding the candle closer. White material, beads and lace—it looked like a wedding gown. Now, who in the world...?

Wait a minute. The closet door hadn't been open when he'd come into the room, had it? There was definitely someone in the house with him—someone who had either arrived in a wedding gown or was preparing to put one on.

Suddenly he realized what this had to be.

"Damn you, Mitchell," Kam breathed, groaning and shaking his head. "This isn't funny."

His brother had set this up. He had no doubt about it. Mitch was always playing tricks—and always trying to throw women at him. He should never have told the brat he was heading out to the Big Island and his beach house to recuperate from an especially difficult case he'd just finished trying in Honolulu. He'd told Mitch he was coming out to his beach house for peace and quiet. And obviously, Mitchell, meddling younger brother that he was, had taken it upon himself to provide his older brother with some company.

Great. Now he had a woman to get rid of before he could begin to relax. But where was she hiding? He was in no mood for cat-and-mouse games.

Shifting the candle, he started out into the hall, looking to either side and then going into the living room. Shadows lurched awkwardly from the flickering candlelight, making him see movement where there was none. He stopped and tried to listen for the sounds of stealth, but the rain was still pounding and it could have masked the noise of a whole herd of brides.

"Or maybe *bevy* is the word," he muttered to himself as he glanced behind a tall chair and then squinted at the dark place behind the couch. Did brides come in bevies? It was a question to ponder on some later date, when he had time to snooze in the sun and muse upon trivial dilemmas. Right now he had to find the stowaway and restore the sanctity of his castle, such as it was.

Traveling back down the hall, he gave a cursory look in the kitchen and then sudden instinct drew him back to the bedroom where the gown lay. The window was still partly open.

A shadow sank back into the closet just as he entered, and he held the candle high.

"Hold it right there. I can see you."

The shadow didn't move. This was getting really annoying. Stepping forward, he reached in and firmly gripped something thin but evidently attached to the woman in question and pulled her out into the candlelight.

At first glance she looked like a ragamuffin, her wiry blond hair curling wildly around her face, her blue eyes defiant. He was reminded, momentarily, of cockney urchins in Victorian London—the sort the upper-class gentlemen always seemed to be taking by the scruff of the neck, amid much kicking and yelling.

"Touch me again," she growled at him, breaking free of his grasp, though she didn't try to run for it, "and I'll call the police."

Kam blinked at her impertinence. "*You'll* call the police? Whose house is this, anyway?"

"You tell me," she said boldly, her chin jutting out as though she were the aggrieved party. "You're the one who came barging in out of the storm. How do I know you belong here anymore than I do?"

He frowned. The woman had spirit. Too bad he despised women with spirit. But he had to give grudging admiration to this one's attempt to put him on the defensive. "At least you admit you don't belong here," he said pointedly.

"I'm not admitting anything."

"Of course not. Prowlers seldom do."

She hoped her shiver didn't show. She was completely out of line here, and she knew it. He could throw the book at her. "I'm no prowler," she maintained stoutly, though she knew she didn't have a leg to stand on.

"Oh, no?" Despite everything, his mouth twisted into something vaguely resembling a grin. "Then, what would you call yourself?"

"A...visitor." That sounded nice. One wouldn't call the cops on a visitor, would he? Of course not.

"Okay," Kam said shortly. "I'll buy that. As long as you add the word 'uninvited.'"

She was losing some of her defiance now that it was evident he wasn't going to hurt her. "I don't want to get into an argument over semantics," she said evasively. "Is this your house or isn't it?"

"It is."

She hesitated. So calling the cops was still a possibility. "Well . . . nice little place you've got here."

Something in her tone made him lift an eyebrow. "I like it." He smiled sarcastically. "But I take it you're used to something more luxurious?"

Ashley glanced quickly into his dark gaze, wondering how he could tell, and nodded. "Actually, yes. But this does seem quite comfortable."

He wanted to laugh, but he held it back. How about that? A picky housebreaker. She had some nerve. Still, she wasn't really a housebreaker, and he knew it. She was a gift from his brother. And she was about to be returned.

"Listen," he said abruptly. "How much is he paying you?"

She looked at him, startled. "What?"

"Whatever it is, I'll give you double to go away."

She gaped at him in wonder. Did this mean there would be no police, no handcuffs, no leg irons? "Believe me, you don't have to pay to get rid of me. I'll be very happy to go away."

"Okay." Kam shrugged, standing back, his arms folded. "Then go."

"Okay," she responded promptly. "I will."

Yet as she turned toward the doorway, she grimaced, realizing what this meant. It was pouring outside. She was about to get very, very wet. And where in the world was she going to go? Her footsteps began to lag.

"Hey, wait a minute."

She stopped and looked back questioningly. He seemed very tall, looming against the candlelight, his face gaunt, his eyes deep and dark. "Isn't that my shirt?" he asked, squinting at her.

She looked down at herself. "Uh, yes, it is." She flipped back her hair with a casual gesture and looked at him sideways. "Mind if I sort of... borrow it for a while?"

He frowned down at her, looking the part of a disapproving uncle. "You take a lot for granted, lady. Don't you have anything else to wear?"

She shrugged and for the first time her brilliant smile broke out like sunshine from behind a cloud. "One very used wedding gown," she noted with a forlorn shake of her head.

"Used, huh?" Kam noticed the smile, but he was used to resisting that sort of thing. Turning back to the pile of white fabric, he poked at it with his foot. "What did you do, come from the airport in it?"

Ashley cocked her head to the side as she regarded him. He seemed to have a very fixed idea as to who she was and what she was doing here, and she wasn't at all sure what that might be. "Not exactly," she said tentatively.

He sighed and threw her a befuddled glance. "A woman in a wedding dress. You and Mitch have a pretty weird idea of what might appeal to me."

Mitch. Who the heck was Mitch? He really did think he had her pegged. The only problem was, he had her pegged all wrong. She frowned. "Look, I don't know who you think I am—"

"Don't worry about it," Kam said hastily. "I think you're probably an out-of-work actress," he said, giving her the benefit of the doubt, "who needed a little cash and took the job."

This was ridiculous and she might as well stop him right there. "I'm no actress," she protested.

His wide grin flashed. "Well, I wasn't going to say anything, but I have to admit, you haven't exactly been bowling me over."

"No kidding," she said tartly. "Though I've been charged with trying to be a comedienne in my time, no one has ever accused me of being an actress before."

"A comedienne, are you?" he said, taking her much too literally. "Same thing, just about."

"Hardly." She frowned at him, perplexed. Didn't the man recognize sarcasm when he heard it?

"Well, Mitch always says I have no sense of humor, and maybe he's right."

Ashley blinked at him, wondering if he could possibly be for real. He took everything so darn seriously. But at least he wasn't going to turn her in to the authorities, so she supposed she ought to be thankful. Though it was a little difficult conjuring up a sense of gratitude when all she had to look forward to was a wet, rainy night with nowhere to hide.

She looked out the window at the rain. Maybe she would have to go back. What would they say? What would Wesley do? She could see his triumphant look right now.

"Ha," he would say with a sneer. "Thought you could go out on your own, did you? Just see what a mess you make of it. You're much better off marrying me. At least you'll be taken care of. You need a full-time keeper, Ashley. You haven't got the wits to come in from the rain."

And maybe he was right. She shivered and looked at the tall man holding the candle. "I guess I'd better get going," she said in a small, forlorn voice. Taking a deep breath, she turned again. "Don't worry," she said. "I promise I'll get your shirt back to you."

She was going. Good. In a moment things would be back to normal—nice and quiet, the way he liked them. But Kam took another look at her bare legs and that ridiculous shirt, and he knew he couldn't let her go this way.

"Wait a minute." He joined her in the hallway. "Don't you have a coat or anything?"

She shook her head.

He grimaced. This was impossible and they both knew it, but he still stalled for time. "Where are you going to go?"

She looked at him curiously. "What does it matter to you?"

He hesitated. "I could loan you a coat. And give you a ride back to the airport, if you want."

"I'm not going to the airport."

Lightning flashed, illuminating the hall for a brief moment. She stared at him, draped in silver, looking like an apparition in the night. He looked back and saw a waif about to be cast out into the storm.

Kam was supposed to be hard. He was supposed to have no heart. That was what he'd been told. But he'd have to be a real monster to cast even a dog out on a night like this. And he wasn't a monster. Not yet.

Swearing softly, he took a step that positioned him between her and the back door. "It seems this storm isn't going to let up anytime soon." He shook his head, giving in to his better instincts. What else could he do?

"Hell with it, you might as well stay here tonight. You can go back in the morning. Then you can tell Mitch anything you want. Tell him we had an orgy. That'll make him happy."

She froze, not sure she liked the sound of that. Her fingers went to the opening in the shirt. Maybe it would be better to brave the storm, after all. "What?"

"Sure." Kam grinned, suddenly enjoying himself as he held the candle high and led the way to the kitchen. "Tell him the moment I saw you I was consumed with desire. Tell him I threw you down on the kitchen table...." He made a sweeping motion toward that very object, making her jump. "That I had my way with you before we'd even been properly introduced. That making love ignited a fever in us both, that we thrashed it out all night long, and you had to leave early the next morning because you couldn't take any more." He chuckled, setting the candle down on the counter. "Tell him all that. Let him have it. He deserves it."

Ashley shrank back against the stove, wide-eyed and estimating the distance to the back door, a door she'd already tried and found locked. She wasn't a bit pleased with the turn the conversation had taken. "You know," she said tentatively, "I really think it would be better if I just left now."

"What?" Kam turned, frowning. Why was she acting like this? What was she upset about? It couldn't be his little joke about throwing her down on the kitchen table, could it? After all, what was she doing here if not to provide female companionship of the intimate sort? And yet, here she was acting the part of the shrinking violet. He turned away, annoyed and a little embarrassed, though he would never have admitted it to anyone.

"Don't be ridiculous," he said gruffly. "Of course, you'll stay. After all, I'm sure you assumed I'd let you stay from the beginning, didn't you?"

She hesitated, but he turned to frown at her and went right on, shaking a stern finger her way. "But that's all. Let's get one thing straight. Mitchell was the playboy in the family. One-night stands are not my style."

That was a relief. She straightened, brightening. "Mine, either," she said promptly.

He threw her a quizzical look. Then, what was she doing here? Who was she trying to kid, anyway? "Right," he said skeptically, looking her up and down. "Listen, you can stay, but just for tonight."

She sneezed and he grimaced.

"There's no way I can let you go out in that flimsy shirt. Sit down. I'll make us both a pot of tea."

She sank warily into a seat at the breakfast nook. A man who wanted to fix her tea couldn't be all bad, could he? If he had designs, he would be more likely to break out the brandy. Clenching her hands together on the table in front of her, she watched as he lit the fire and prepared the tea bags, then poured out the hot liquid once it had boiled.

"Thank you," she said when he'd handed her a cup and slid into a seat across from her. She took a tentative sip and felt the soothing liquid slide down and do its magic on her nervous system. "How long do you think the electricity will stay off?"

"There's no telling. We're sort of primitive over here on this end of the island. We don't get much attention from the authorities, or the utilities. That's what I like about it."

That was what she'd liked, too, until she'd ended up stranded in a dark house with a stranger.

"What's your name?" he asked.

She hesitated. There might be something on the news about her. But, what the heck? With no electricity, he wouldn't know anyway. "Ashley Carrington. What's yours?"

"Kam Caine." He raised an eyebrow. "But you know that already, don't you?"

Did she? He seemed to think she should. She didn't answer. Instead, she looked around the room. "Is this your vacation house?" she asked.

He nodded. "I practice law in Honolulu," he said casually. "I've had one rough case after another these last few months. So I came out to get a little rest and relaxation." He grimaced. "Unfortunately, I told Mitchell I was coming."

"Oh."

He hesitated. "I don't mean to be rude. Don't take it personally. But I can choose my own feminine companionship. I don't need Mitchell setting me up." He half grinned as he looked her over. "His taste is completely different from mine."

She stared at him, appalled. Was a man like this just born this charming, or did he have to work at it as he grew? "So I don't appeal to you, is that it?" She almost laughed out loud. As if she cared!

Kam shrugged. "No offense, but you're just a little small for me." He surveyed her dispassionately. "I like tall women. Women with a little . . . class and bearing."

She choked. "I see. So you think I have no class."

He made a quick face and shook his head. "I didn't say that."

She gave him a mock glare. "Do you deny you were thinking it?"

His face went hard and cold and all expression left his glittering green eyes. "I don't have to deny anything."

She grinned. "Spoken like a true bloodsucking lawyer."

His face didn't change, but his eyes hardened. "Hey, now who's getting personal?"

"I am." She sighed. The man was impossible and she wasn't sure why she should bother to explain the world to him. He wasn't going to understand anyway. But, what the heck?

"Listen, how do you think I feel?" she told him. "You're rejecting me. You seem to think I came to be your bimbo, and you're telling me I just don't turn you on. I'm crushed," she added, sarcasm dripping from her tongue.

Kam gazed at her as though she were speaking a foreign language. This wasn't at all the way a woman like this was supposed to act. "I'm sorry, but that's just the way it is." He laughed shortly. "Listen, you haven't exactly fallen for me like a ton of bricks, either, have you? We're just not a match. Leave it at that."

She hesitated. She really ought to tell him the truth. This masquerade had come close to getting out of hand. But suddenly sleepy from the tea, she was just too tired to fight his misapprehension. It had been a long day of preparing to get married with all the folderol that accompanied that, to wondering if she should escape, to actually hightailing it out of the church and running as though demons were chasing her, to breaking in here and then being scared out of her wits when the owner came home unexpectedly. She needed sleep and she needed it soon.

"I'm sorry to be a bother to you, Mr. Caine," she said groggily. "If you could just show me where I can sleep, I'll get some rest and be on my way as soon as possible in the morning."

"Oh."

Was it her imagination or did he look disappointed that they wouldn't get a longer chat?

"Sure. Come on into the living room. I'll get some blankets and pillows and we'll fix you up on the sofa. There's no bed in the second bedroom."

She followed the bobbing circle of light and soon found herself ensconced on the living room couch with a pillow and a light comforter tucked in around her.

"Good night," she murmured, her eyelids drooping.

"Night," he muttered back, frowning down at her. This was some strange chick Mitchell had tossed his way. But he would be rid of her first thing in the morning. No problem.

Two

It must have been a slash of lightning that woke her. She wasn't sure what it had been, but suddenly she was shaking with fear, and every shadow in the room looked menacing.

She told herself it was silly to feel this way. She knew there was nothing in the room that could hurt her. Then another flash of lightning cracked the sky, and she saw a man's face outside the window.

Wesley. He'd come to drag her back. The breath stopped in her throat.

And then it started again. That wasn't Wesley, and she was being a total fool. It was just a young palm tree. There, she could really see it now. No Wesley at all. She could calm back down.

But she couldn't. The room just became more and more intimidating. The wind, the rain, the shifting light, everything combined to make her uncertain in what she saw, what she heard. She hated herself for being such a ninny, but she was truly scared.

Rising off the couch, she gathered her covers around her and headed for the bedroom, stepping lightly. Her heart was beating and she was sure some shadow would turn into a beast from the underworld at any moment, but she managed to keep herself in check and walked into Kam's bedroom without making a sound. Silently she settled in the chair beside his bed, curling into it and pulling the covers around her. And finally she glanced over at him.

He looked very large, lying still under the covers, one arm wrapped around the pillow under his head. Her pulse began to quiet. It was going to be okay. Nothing was going to happen here. She sank lower into the chair and sighed. Now if only she could go to sleep again.

But sleep wasn't going to come anytime soon. She could feel it. Every nerve ending was still quivering. And her mind was shifting into overdrive. She was going to think furiously for a while, think about all the things she shouldn't have done, all the things she should have but didn't, all the things that might happen if she didn't watch out.

Ashley certainly had plenty to think about. It wasn't every day one ran away from her own wedding. On the dark side of midnight, it seemed an incredibly stupid thing to have done. How was she ever going to live this one down?

"What's the matter?" Kam was awake, his head raised above the pillow, and he'd seen her. "What are you doing here?"

Ashley stirred uncomfortably. "I'm sorry. I didn't mean to wake you."

He frowned in the dark, just able to make out the features of her face in the silver light that changed as the wind slashed into the trees outside the window.

"Is something wrong?" he asked.

"No. I don't want to bother you. Just . . . keep on sleeping."

He raised himself up on his elbow. "You think I can sleep with you sitting there staring at me?" he demanded.

"I won't stare, I promise. It's just . . ." What was it, and how could she possibly explain to him when she could hardly explain it to herself? "I need to be close to another human being right now. I can't help it."

He stared at her, wondering if she was as kooky as she sounded, or if this was some sort of come-on. Then he noticed that she was shivering uncontrollably. He rose, swinging his legs down over the side of the bed, keeping the sheet wrapped around his hips.

"Are you cold?" he asked, incredulous, for despite the fast-fading storm, the night was quite warm.

"No," she denied vehemently. "No, really, I'll be okay if you just let me stay here. I won't make a sound, I promise. Just go back to sleep."

There were tears on her face. He could see the reflections in the moonlight. What did that mean? Had he hurt her somehow? He was always affecting women in ways he didn't expect or didn't mean to. He didn't understand them. Kam felt helpless and annoyed, as though a puppy had woken him and now needed attention, and all he wanted to do was go back to sleep. But that darn puppy had such an appealing face. . . .

"Why are you crying?" he asked her abruptly.

She turned, startled. "I'm not," she said defensively.

"Then, what's that wet stuff on your face?"

She quickly wiped her cheeks with the back of her hand and sniffed. "It's nothing. I wish you'd ignore me and go back to sleep."

Easier said than done.

"Close your eyes," he ordered sternly.

She stared at him, wide-eyed. "What for?"

"I want to get up," he told her. "And I don't have anything on."

"Oh." She had a ridiculous urge to giggle, but she stifled it. "I can't see anything in the dark."

"I don't care. Close your eyes, anyway."

She complied, putting an arm over her face and squeezing her eyes tightly closed, silently chuckling all the while at the surprising modesty of the man.

Getting up off the bed, he made his way to his dresser, pulling out the top drawer and rummaging until he found a pair of pajama bottoms, which he hastily tugged on.

"Wait right here," he said gruffly. "I'll get you a glass of milk. I picked up some on the way back from the airport. That'll put you back to sleep."

"I don't need anything," she protested faintly as he disappeared into the hallway. She dropped her arm and sighed. She hated milk. But it was a nice thought.

He was back in no time, carrying a glass for each of them. "Here," he said, handing one to her. "Drink up. Don't worry, it's cold. The electricity is back on."

She found herself smiling in the dark. "Aren't you going to turn on the light?" she suggested.

"No," he said shortly as he sat down on the edge of the bed. "When you turn on the light, you admit you're not going back to sleep again anytime soon. And I'm not ready to admit that just yet."

"I'm sorry," she said in a small voice, cupping the glass in her hands but not drinking. "I know I'm being a pain in the neck, but I just got so scared, I had to come in here and be closer."

She was shivering again. He frowned, wondering what was wrong with her.

"Do you need another blanket?" he asked.

She shook her head. "No, thanks. I'm okay, really." She set down the untouched glass of milk on the night table. "It's just been an emotional day for me."

"Oh." He relaxed a little. At least that probably meant it had nothing to do with him. "It's been a pretty weird one for me, too."

He thought about Jerry's face that afternoon in court, how the defense attorney had been purple with rage, so angry he'd spewed saliva all over Kam as he'd yelled at him.

"What are you doing to my client?" he'd yelled. "Have you no compassion? Have you no heart? Is there any blood in those icy veins, or are you some sort of android made to twist human beings until you get the last drop out of them?"

Jerry had grabbed Kam by the lapels. "You're killing me, you bastard," he'd cried in a voice that had come straight from his gut. "You're killing me. And you don't give a damn, do you?"

The voice echoed in his head, mocking him. And the funny thing was, he didn't give a damn. Jerry was right. Kam had no heart. Not anymore. He'd found, over time, that it didn't pay to have one.

Still, Jerry's tirade had bothered him enough to send him off for a bit of rest and recuperation. He was way overdue for a vacation, and he'd decided, suddenly, to go ahead and take one, even if it was just for a long weekend. He'd counted on the solitude of his beach house. He hadn't known he would have company right from the get-go.

"One thing still puzzles me," he said, sipping his milk, his eyes narrowed in the gloom. "Why did you and Mitchell think a girl in a wedding gown would turn me on?"

She sighed and turned toward him. It was about time she got this over with.

"I have to tell you something," she said softly. "I don't know anybody named Mitchell."

It took a while for the full implication of that admission to sink in. He sat, blinking quietly, wondering how she could have meant what she had just said.

"What?" he asked at last, seeking clarification that would set things straight.

"I should have told you right from the beginning, but you seemed so happy with your version of things. I wasn't sent here by anybody." It felt good to get this out in the open, even though she had a feeling he wasn't going to like it at all. "I came in through your back window because I needed a place to stay for the night."

He stared at her in the darkness. Okay, things were finally coming clear for him. She hadn't been hired by his brother to make his life miserable. He'd moved to a new level. Now people were making his life miserable for free.

"Then you're just a . . . a common criminal, and I have no responsibility toward you whatsoever."

She nodded and shrugged, feeling guilty, but relieved. "That's right."

He recoiled, swearing softly to himself. Oh, brother. He felt like a sucker, and he hated feeling that way. His first impulse had been the right one. He should have thrown her out right from the beginning.

But maybe it wasn't too late.

"I should call the police," he said coolly, eyes burning. "They'll give you a warm and dry place to sleep tonight."

She shivered. "If you want to call the police, go ahead. But..."

"But what?" he growled.

Her voice sounded soft and woebegone. "I wish you wouldn't."

He wasn't going to, at least not until morning, but he wasn't about to admit that to her. That would be much too easy.

"Well, let's hear it all," he said gruffly. "What the hell are you doing here in my house? Why did you break in?"

She hesitated, staring dreamily into space. "I was supposed to get married tonight," she said softly.

Thus the wedding gown. He nodded in the dark. "What happened?"

"I ran away just before the ceremony."

"You what?" She was obviously crazy. No sane person would do such a thing. "No, you didn't," he said accusingly. "People just don't do things like that."

Her laugh was soft and sad. "I did."

That made him angry for some reason, and he wasn't sure of the cause. "Why?" he asked, actually requesting understanding he wasn't likely to get, as much as information.

Why? Yes, that was the big question. Had she really asked it of herself yet? Had she answered it in any rational way? She wasn't really sure.

"I suddenly realized it was all a big mistake" was all she told him.

He turned away, mouth twisted with cynicism. She was a complete flake. That much was obvious. He hated women like her. There was no logic to their behavior. They jumped from one thing to another with no rhyme or reason to their changes of mood. He liked things orderly, with motivations in place. He understood motivations. At least, he understood the sort he dealt with most often in court. The motivations that drove women were forever a dark conundrum to him. Women, on the whole, were shadowy mysteries.

"So you just left your fiancé standing there, waiting for you?" he said accusingly.

She nodded. It was going to be hard to make him understand. "I tried to tell him. I'd been trying to tell him for a week, but he wouldn't listen to me."

He grunted his skepticism. "The direct approach might have worked. Maybe, if you'd had a little guts, if you'd handed back his ring and told him face-to-face...."

Ashley turned toward Kam, trying to see his eyes, but all she could make out was the outline of him sitting on the side of the bed. "But I did," she protested. "I did exactly that. And everyone laughed and assumed I was joking."

"I see." Just as he'd thought. A flake. Those closest to her should know. "I'll bet you're known for your sense of humor, aren't you?" he said, not making it sound like a compliment. "A regular little cutup, aren't you?"

"Something like that." She grimaced, not wanting to go into it too deeply. There had been a time when she'd been considered the life of every party. But those days were long gone.

He put down his empty glass with a thump. So she'd left her dearly beloved standing at the altar, all because she'd changed her mind.

Women! What was it with them, anyway? Did they enjoy the sense of power they held over men? No woman was ever going to have any power over him—

not again. He'd found out the hard way just how painful that could be.

"So, who is this man you were planning to marry?" The question was asked idly. Though he knew this part of the island from having grown up nearby, he never expected to recognize any name she might throw out.

"His name's Wesley," she began. "I—"

"Wesley Butler?" His head snapped around. "You're kidding."

She was as surprised as he was. "Do you know him?"

"Yeah, I know him." Reaching out, he snapped on the light so he could take a better look at her. She blinked up at him from where she was snuggled down in the chair, covers tucked securely around her, and he frowned. She looked more guileless than ever, with her huge blue eyes and her blond hair flying out around her face in ethereal wisps. She really didn't strike him as Wesley's type at all. "What would you want to marry a jerk like that for?" he said bluntly.

She gave a start, then burst out laughing. "That is precisely the point," she noted with delight. "Once I got here and was thrown in with him night and day, I realized I didn't want to marry him at all."

If he wasn't careful he was going to be tempted to smile back at her, and he didn't want to do that. He wanted to maintain a lot of distance from this one. Something told him he was going to need it.

"How do you know Wesley?" she asked, glad for the light so that she could see his eyes. "Did you go to school with him?"

"School?" He grimaced. "Not quite. Wesley went to the best academies available. I went to public school, along with the other peons."

"Oh." She bit her lip. She'd gone to only the "best" herself, but she thought she might keep that quiet for the moment. He seemed to have some sort of resentment toward people with money. She'd noticed that before.

"I knew Wesley from swim team," he went on. "We both swam for the YMCA team during the summer." He leaned back, remembering. "We were about thirteen, fourteen, I guess. Wesley and I always competed for the backstroke slot in the medley relay."

"Who usually won?"

"Most of the time I did." His gaze hardened as he looked into the past. "When push comes to shove, I don't let anybody beat me," he mused, almost to himself.

Watching him, she suppressed a shiver. He had a cold streak in him, an inner core of steel that would be hard to bend. She was going to have to keep that in mind.

He turned back to her and the present. "How did you two meet?" he asked shortly.

"Our families have been friends forever and ever. He used to spend vacations with us in La Jolla sometimes."

Uh-oh. She'd pretty much given away her own background, hadn't she? Glancing into his eyes, she tried to see how he was taking what she was telling him, but his face was impassive, his eyes hard as glass. "Then we both ended up going to the same East Coast university," she said. "He was a senior when I was a freshman, and he took me under his wing."

"You went to college?"

He acted surprised, and she looked at him, amused rather than offended.

"Yes, I went to college. I went to several of them, in fact."

"Couldn't make up your mind?"

"No. Actually I got kicked out of the first one."

"Sneaking a boyfriend into the dorm?"

She laughed. "They don't frown on that any longer. Hadn't you heard? No, what happened was, as a freshman, I joined an animal activist group, because, after all, I do like animals and don't want to hear of anyone being mean to them."

He groaned. "Here it comes," he said.

"Yes. We slunk out in the dark of night and let all the rats and bunnies go from the experimental lab." She sighed. "What a farce that was. Half the bunnies, who'd never been free before and didn't have a clue, got hit by cars, and I'm sure the rats had a wonderful time invading the neighborhood, but I imagine the neighbors weren't too happy and took retaliatory measures soon thereafter."

"And you got caught."

"Yup. And expelled. A move I am in complete agreement with now. It only took doing volunteer work in a children's terminal ward to teach me the value of experimental medicine. When it comes to a choice between children and rats, I'm on the side that wants to save the kids."

It was beginning to dawn on him just what a strange one he had here in his house. He frowned. From what she'd said, he assumed she was from a family just as wealthy as Wesley's. And yet she'd climbed into his little tacky beach house to run away from it all. Slumming. Wasn't that what they called it?

She and Wesley had grown up together, had gone to the same university. He hadn't seen Wesley in all this time, but he'd heard he was still the same bastard he'd always been.

"So you two went to school together," Kam said musingly. "That must have been quite a while ago."

She threw back her head and laughed. He really didn't pull any punches, did he? She wasn't sure if she was going to like that quality in the long run. But, what the heck? There wasn't going to be any long run. Right now, it just made her laugh.

"Well, I guess you told me," she teased. "And here I was hoping to make you think I was a dewy-eyed, twenty-year-old."

He snorted, completely uninterested in soothing any feathers. "Dewy you may be, but I wouldn't say you were vacant and giggly."

She grinned. "You think all twenty-year old women are vacant and giggly?"

"Most of the ones I've come in contact with have been."

"And you hate vacant and giggly women," she guessed.

"You might say that."

"I might," she agreed, regarding him levelly. "Or I might go a step further and say you hate more than that. Like the entire female side of the gender wars."

He grimaced, but there was a slight smile curling his lips. "I wouldn't go quite that far," he drawled. "Still, I've got to admit, I don't like the games women play."

"Games." She only wished it were only a game. When it affected your whole life, your whole sense of yourself, it had to be more than a game. In any case, she knew she'd lost, whatever it was.

"Anyway, I'm cheating," he admitted dryly. "I can guess how old you are, because I know how old Wesley is. Don't take it personally."

Don't take it personally. She had a feeling that was a common catch phrase with him. He had an air of reserve and distance from any sort of emotional entanglement. He wouldn't get mad. But he would definitely get even.

"So, tell me what happened," he prompted. "What gave you the clue that Wesley was not really good husband material?"

She pulled the covers up against her neck. She didn't really want to talk about this, but she supposed she owed him that much, at least. After all, he'd taken her in when she'd been desperate. She was still desperate. But maybe he couldn't tell.

"It started out nicely enough," she said softly, looking back at the week before. "Wesley's family have such a beautiful house. That view of the ocean...."

Kam grunted. "Pretty impressive, if you like over-done opulence."

She glanced his way. There it was again, that slight sense of resentment toward rich people. She wondered where he'd gotten that. "I was impressed. And everything was all right until my family arrived."

"They came for the wedding?"

She nodded. "You see, my mother was here with her new boyfriend, and my father was here with his new girlfriend, and no one was paying any attention...."

The picture was coming in loud and clear. She'd expected to be the center of attention at her own wedding and when that didn't pan out, she'd stamped her foot and had a tantrum. And then she'd run away.

"You're a spoiled little rich girl, aren't you?" he said with mild scorn. "No one was paying court, so you figured out a way to get the spotlight back. Like a little girl holding her breath and turning blue. Like a little boy threatening to go eat some worms."

"I'm not spoiled," she said with sincere indignation. How could she be spoiled when no one ever noticed her? "It wasn't attention I wanted."

"Then what was it?"

That was a very good question. Right now, she couldn't answer it.

"So you had your tantrum," he said coolly. "You ran off and landed here. What's next?"

"I—I'm not sure."

She wasn't sure. Great. A woman on the loose without a plan. It sounded to him as though the best thing for her would be to go home and face the music. That was what any normal person would do. She didn't have to hide out to avoid marrying Wesley, did she? Of course not. All she had to do was develop a little backbone and tell the people who loved her what was what.

"Meanwhile, your family is probably worried sick," he reminded her. "They're probably combing the countryside for you."

She shook her head, almost wistful. "No. I doubt it. I called and left a message that I was okay. Besides, they're probably still at the reception."

"Reception?" He stared at her. "What reception? How can there be a reception when there was no wedding?"

She laughed aloud. "Are you kidding? The reception was already paid for. My mother would never let a good party go to waste."

Despite the laugh, Kam could hear the real pain in Ashley's voice, and for the first time he began to think there might be more to her side of things than he'd first thought.

But that didn't matter. He didn't want to hear about it. They'd spent enough time chatting. She'd calmed down and now, maybe, she would let him get some sleep. In the morning, things would look better. Things might even make sense.

Reaching out, he switched off the light.

"Good night," she said.

He turned and looked at where her figure loomed in the dark. "What are you going to do in the morning?" he asked.

There was a long pause. "I don't know," she said at last.

"Well, you can't stay here," he told her sternly, just to make sure she wasn't counting on anything. "You'll have to find another place to hide."

"I know." She sighed, snuggling down deeper into the chair. "Don't worry. I'll be out of your hair in no time."

That she would. She could count on it. Content now that they had that straight, he closed his eyes and drifted quickly into sleep, breathing evenly.

Ashley sat very still and watched him. She couldn't go to sleep. Turmoil still churned inside her. Something about the easy way he fell asleep, the total relaxation of his body, comforted her. She wished she could touch him. Maybe some of that calm would rub off on her.

The clouds were mostly gone now, and a full moon reigned. The wind was whipping the trees around just outside the windows, making wild, eerie shadows on the walls of the room. The outside world was still in pandemonium. And so was the world inside her heart.

She should lose this aching anxiety and find herself some peace. But how could she? She had wrecked everything, all her hopes and dreams, all her mother's plans, her father's schemes. There would be no going back. Surely Wesley wouldn't even want her now, after what she'd done, how she'd humiliated him in front of all his friends and family.

Not that she wanted to go back. No, she couldn't do that. But she was sorry—sorry she'd ruined everyone's conception of how things would be, sorry she'd hurt Wesley, sorry she'd let this thing snowball until it was running wild, destroying her own vision of finally having something to call hers.

She was shivering again. She knew it wasn't cold, knew it was just her nerves. But the feeling of desolation that swept through her was as real as anything she'd ever felt before. She looked longingly at where Kam slept, and then she knew what she had to do.

He wasn't going to like this. She would try to be very, very quiet and not wake him. Slowly, and as softly as she could, she slid out of the chair and crept into his bed. He moved, and she held her breath, her shoulders scrunched as though prepared for a blow. But he settled back down again, and she let the breath out slowly.

She'd known he would be warm. She got as close as she dared. She could hear his breathing, feel his warmth, but she didn't dare touch him. Still, she could feel herself begin to relax, feel the tension begin to melt away. He was big and male and very comforting. For the first time since she'd run from the church, she felt safe. Sighing, she stretched out.

Suddenly he was rolling over. She tried to avoid him, but he was too quick, and then he had flung his arm across her shoulder, and it stayed there, fingers trailing her collarbone.

The shock rolled away as she realized he was still asleep. The feel of his touch was like magic. She'd known it would be.

What was it about him that was so comforting? She wasn't sure. Maybe it had something to do with his rocklike personality. He wasn't one to give with the wind, that was for sure. And right now she felt like she needed someone like that. There had been too much agitation in her life lately.

She smiled, and her eyelids drifted down. In less than a heartbeat, she was asleep herself.

Three

Kam was dreaming. That had to be it. He was dreaming of softness and a scent that made him want to hold something. And then he woke up and began to take in the room around him.

For one long moment he stared at his own hand with a growing sense of horror. His hand was on her shoulder. Ashley was in his bed. This wasn't the way it had been when he'd fallen asleep. What the hell was going on here?

Sunlight was streaming in through the window. It was late. He was usually up at the crack of dawn. How could he have slept right through her climbing into bed with him?

She looked even smaller in the morning light, her hair spilling out over his pillow, her dark lashes lying long and curved against her cheeks. What she looked was vulnerable—and he wanted no part of her.

He pulled back his hand as steadily as possible, breathing a sigh of relief when she didn't seem to waken. Then he began to inch his way backward, out of the bed.

A sound stopped him. Frozen with shock, he heard his name being called from the living room.

"Kam? Don't tell me you're not up yet."

He groaned. There just wasn't any end to this run of bad luck, was there?

Ashley had heard it, too. Awake now, she was staring up at him, a strange wildness in her eyes.

"Who...?" Ashley began.

He shook his head, his finger to his lips. "It's my sister, Shawnee," he told her quietly, looking down at the golden picture she made against the white sheets. "Unfortunately, she has a key. Stay here. I'll see what she wants."

He wished he had time to change into jeans, but he didn't. The longer he lingered, the more chance he'd have Shawnee right in here with them. And that wouldn't do. That wouldn't do at all. So he went out in the pajama bottoms, feeling like a fool, hurrying, and as a result, stubbing his toe on the doorframe and swearing obscenely as he hopped into the living room on one foot.

"Watch your language," his sister told him primly. "I've brought company."

And she had, indeed. Kam stared in dismay at the pretty young thing trailing into his house behind Shawnee. She looked shy, sweet, slightly overwhelmed and definitely embarrassed to be meeting a man in his pajamas.

But Shawnee didn't seem to notice. Throwing her arms around her brother, she kissed him soundly and leaned back to look lovingly at his face.

"You look terrible," she announced with a sort of sisterly satisfaction. "It's a good thing you came home. We'll get you fixed up in no time."

Turning, she pulled her young friend closer. "Kam, this is Melissa Kim. She's my new assistant manager at the café. We just happened to be passing by, and I told her she ought to come in and meet my little brother." She gave him a significant look that was as good as a wink.

Kam looked into the green, laughing eyes of the sister he loved and contemplated a quick, tidy little murder. Ever since he'd turned thirty she'd been showing up with girls he might be interested in. Shawnee told everyone she was determined to see him married. It was getting to be a real pain in the neck.

"Nice to meet you, Melissa," he mumbled, giving her the briefest of smiles. "Listen, Shawnee, it's great to see you, but..."

Shawnee turned, taking in the room, her long braid bouncing against her spine. Every bit of body language she possessed told him she was here for a reason, and she wasn't going to leave until that reason had been fulfilled. "It's so nice having you back here on the Big Island," she said breezily. "Mitchell told me you were coming home for a little vacation, and I started making plans right away. The first thing on my agenda was to come by and say hi."

"Hi back," he responded dutifully as she grinned at him. "Uh, thanks for coming by."

Hesitating, he made up his mind. He was going to try it. He had to. He didn't want to meet Melissa, he didn't want to have to turn down whatever scheme Shawnee had in mind. And most of all, he didn't want the two of them seeing the woman he had in his bedroom at that very moment.

Running a hand through his tousled hair, he gave them both a sheepish smile, meant to be persuasive.

"But you know," he said, "I got in awfully late last night, and there was that storm and the electricity went out and... to tell you the truth, I'm still half asleep, so—"

Shawnee's chin lifted at the challenge. "Oh, Kam, don't you worry about a thing. Look what we brought along."

She lifted two white sacks for his inspection. "Coffee and doughnuts, sweetheart, just like you like them." She jerked her head toward the doorway. "Come on, let's go into the kitchen. We can have a little chat and have our breakfast at the same time."

She started for the kitchen, but he grabbed her arm and pulled her back. "Shawnee, wait," he said softly, just for her ears. "I'm not dressed."

She made a face, as though that didn't mean a thing. "It's morning, darling. No one expects you to be dressed." She took his hand and tugged at it. "Come on."

Smiling beguilingly, she began to pull him toward the kitchen. "Now you just come on in and sit down. We're planning to ply you with food and drink and maybe get you to come with us to Kona. We're going on a shopping trip."

"Shawnee—"

Protesting all the way, he was maneuvered into the kitchen where she deftly pushed him back into the breakfast nook. "Now, don't you mind Melissa," she said confidently, glancing at his muscular bare chest. "She doesn't care if you don't have a shirt on, do you, Melissa?"

Melissa may not have cared about that, but she certainly cared about something, and she'd turned beet red by the time she slid into the breakfast nook with

Kam. He glared at his sister, trying to send her a message, but she was having none of it.

Why was it, Kam was thinking as Shawnee chattered on, pulling out the cups of coffee and setting them before each in turn, that he still did exactly what she told him to? He was a grown man with a professional career, and he acted as though he were still in elementary school whenever Shawnee came around. She'd raised him. She'd been like a mother to him for years. But this was ridiculous.

The habits of a lifetime were hard to break. But he was a fool to let her order him around like a kid. Maybe it was time to rebel. Good idea. He'd have to try it. Narrowing his eyes, he waited for Shawnee to pause for breath.

"...And you should really see that new theater at the Shangri-la Hotel. They're playing a film noir retrospective right now." She smiled innocently. "Say, you know what? Melissa told me as we were driving over here that she's never seen any film noir. You ought to get together and check it out at the Shangri-la."

Kam put down his coffee cup and glared at her. "No," he said loud and clear.

She stared at him, surprise widening her eyes. "No?" she repeated.

"No," he said again, being very firm. "I'm sick of film noir." He smiled blandly, but as he leaned forward, his eyes were glittering dangerously. "I'm into slice-and-dice flicks now, Shawnee. The bloodier, the better."

She stared for a second, then her face relaxed in a laugh. "Oh, you are not." She waved a hand at him, brushing off his statement. "I know you better than that." She glanced at Melissa, who didn't seem to be quite getting what was going on here. "Never mind, if you're not in the mood for movies. There's going to be a family picnic at Uncle Mahi's Sunday. Are you coming?''

It was a cinch she was ready to invite poor Melissa. "Can't make it," he said shortly.

Shawnee's eyes narrowed. "Mack and Shelley are coming over Monday for dinner—"

This time he didn't even let her finish her sentence. "Going to be busy," he interjected coolly.

Shawnee's mouth twitched and the lower lip began to protrude a bit. "Doing what?" she demanded, chin jutting.

"Resting," he challenged back, matching chin for chin.

They stared at one another for a long moment, then Shawnee staged a strategic retreat. "Oh!" She threw up her hands and shook her head. "I can see you're in the mood to be impossible today, so we'll save it for later."

He shrugged, relaxing, happy to have won one for once. "Fine with me."

Shawnee's eyes flashed. She wasn't used to insubordination from her brother. "He just woke up," she told Melissa reassuringly. "Believe me, he gets better as the day goes on."

"Oh, I think he's just fine right now," the girl said, her tone just a little too fervent.

Kam met Shawnee's green eyes, and they both had to work hard to hold back the laughter.

"Oh, well," Shawnee said, giving up gracefully. She glanced at Melissa and decided on one last-ditch effort. "Now you two just talk and get to know each other," she ordered as she slid out of her seat and rose. "I'm going to go powder my nose."

It took a second for the import of her intentions to come clear to Kam. She was going into the other side of the house. Ashley was over there. She couldn't do that.

"No." He half rose in his seat, reaching out as though he could stop her. "Shawnee, no!"

She turned back and made a face at him. "What's the matter, Kam? Think I'll be shocked by the condition of your bathroom?" She laughed. "I raised three brothers and a son, I know what men can do to a room. Don't worry. I can handle it."

He sank slowly back down into his seat as she whirled away. There was no way to stop her. He only hoped Ashley had had the sense to stay in the bedroom. If Shawnee found her... well, all he had to do was listen for the scream. That would tell him what was up.

Melissa stirred at his side. "So, if you don't like film noir, what kind of movies *do* you like?" she asked shyly. "I like romances myself."

He turned back to her with a pained smile. I'm going to kill Shawnee, he thought with quiet satisfaction. They'll never convict me once I explain....

Shawnee was frowning as she walked down the hallway toward the bathroom. Setting her stubborn brother up with women was hard work. Things had been so easy when he'd been little. Of all the boys, he'd always been the one she could talk to, the one who listened to reason and responded accordingly. He wasn't moody and rebellious like her brother Mack, and he wasn't a wiseacre like Mitchell. He was cool and deliberate, and he knew what he wanted.

"Only what he wants is wrong," she muttered to herself. "He thinks he wants to be left alone. And that's not what he needs, at all."

She was just about to step into the bathroom when a sound caught her ear. She stopped, hand on the knob, sure she'd heard something coming from Kam's room. Strange. Turning, she took the few steps it took to reach the door to his bedroom and pushed her way in.

There on the bed sat a slender waif of a woman, her blond hair flying out around her, her tanned legs stretched out straight, her bare feet impossibly small. Looking up, startled, she stared at Shawnee, and that was when Shawnee realized the woman had on nothing but a man's dress shirt.

"Hi," she said, looking Ashley over in wonder.

"Hi," Ashley said back. She coughed and gave her visitor a sunny smile. "You must be Kam's sister."

Shawnee nodded, still stunned. A woman in Kam's bed. Would wonders never cease?

Ashley read her mind and had the grace to look uncomfortable. "It's...it's not what you think," she said quickly.

"Isn't it?" A wide, slow smile took over Shawnee's pretty face. "What a shame."

"No, really," Ashley said earnestly. "We hardly know each other. We're not...I mean, we didn't..." She gestured helplessly toward the bed.

"Okay." Shawnee was still smiling. "If you say so."

Ashley struggled to explain, eager to set things straight. "You see, it was late. And the storm and all. I was just passing by."

Shawnee nodded wisely. "And you decided to come in out of the rain."

Ashley took a breath and shrugged. "Sort of. Well, Kam invited me to stay and I needed a place to sleep, so I sort of...stayed for the night."

"Uh-huh." Shawnee raised an eyebrow. "You neglected to bring along a nightgown, I see."

Ashley glanced down at the shirt she'd forgotten she was wearing and sighed. "Oh, this thing. It was all I could find to wear. Because, well, I—I don't have any clothes.''

"No clothes?" Shawnee's smile was getting wider all the time. "Gee, that's interesting."

Not really. Ashley sighed. It was much more inconvenient than it was interesting. But she couldn't explain without going into the wedding gown problem, and that would lead into Wesley and all the rest, and she didn't really want to advertise her presence here to the world. So Shawnee would have to try to make sense out of all this without some of the facts.

"It's really a problem," she admitted, regarding her lack of clothes. "I'm going to need something to wear, and Kam's clothes don't fit me at all. Do you have any idea where I could get some things? Is there a boutique nearby?"

Shawnee crossed her arms over her chest and cocked her head to the side to examine this girl who had spent the night with her brother. She was very pretty—not at all what she would have thought was Kam's type. The few times he had been interested in women they had invariably been the tall, elegant sort, very reserved, very chic. Except for Ellen. But that was another story entirely. Of course, he didn't even live on the Big Island most of the time, so she had no idea who he had been seeing in Honolulu.

Yes, she was pretty. But something didn't hang together. Maybe it was the eyes that bothered her. They were crystal blue and quite intelligent. So why was she coming across as such an airhead?

"Let me get this straight," she said slowly. "You were just passing by and my brother invited you in to spend the night." She frowned thoughtfully. "Are you old friends or something?"

Ashley shook her head. "That wasn't exactly what I said." But she didn't elaborate.

"Ahh," Shawnee said, waiting to hear more.

Ashley hesitated. "We're not really friends."

Shawnee nodded, still waiting. "Not lovers. Not friends," she murmured.

"No. We're just barely acquaintances." She spread her hands out, palms up, eyes wide with innocent sincerity. "There's no relationship here. Honest."

"Uh-huh." Shawnee glanced again at the rumpled bed, then noted the covers on the chair. "How long are you staying?"

"Oh, I'm leaving right away."

"As soon as you get some clothes, I suppose."

"Right." She nodded vigorously, her blond hair spilling out like sunshine through a crack in the wall. "Exactly."

"Where is it that you're going?"

Ashley opened her mouth to reply, then snapped it shut and shrugged. "I haven't quite made up my mind yet," she said evasively.

"Do you need a job?" Shawnee's eyes brightened at the thought. "I've got an opening for a morning waitress. I own the Puako Café," she added in explanation. "Come by if you decide you'd like the job."

Ashley looked at her, intrigued. A job as a waitress. That might be fun. It would certainly be different. "I might do that."

"Once you get some clothes."

"Right."

Shawnee smiled. "Well, I'll see you later."

Ashley smiled back. "Maybe so."

Shawnee left, biting her lip thoughtfully. In a few minutes she returned to the breakfast nook with a gleam in her eyes.

"Change of plans, Melissa," she said, scooping up some of the remaining doughnuts and shoving them back into the bag. "We've got to get going right away."

"Now?" Melissa glanced at Kam and then back at Shawnee. She'd been dragged here unwillingly at first, but now that she was getting to know Kam, her reluctance to go was palpable.

"What's going on?" Kam asked suspiciously. He knew his sister well, and he knew that gleam in her eyes for what it was. She was up to something.

"Melissa and I are out of here," Shawnee called back as she started for the door. "We've got things to do, places to go, people to see."

He came behind her, glancing into the hallway, wondering what had changed her mind, afraid he knew.

Turning, she gave him a loud kiss on his cheek. "Love you, bro. Glad you're back. See you later."

"'Bye," Melissa said, trailing behind, leaving with regret. "Hope I see you again sometime."

He nodded. "It's been nice meeting you," he said formally, not giving an inch.

She threw him a sad smile and disappeared through the front door, but before he could turn away, Shawnee was back with a pile of clothes in her arms.

"These are for your friend. Oops—" she grinned at him "—acquaintance. I had a bag of old clothes in the back of the car. I was going to take them to the thrift shop, but she might be able to use these." She turned, ready to dash off again. "'Bye now."

"Wait a minute," Kam said, staring down at the clothes he was now holding. "What friend?"

"You know who I mean." Her grin was irrepressible. "The girl in your bed, you rascal."

"The girl in my..." He blanched. There was no other word for it. Ashley had still been in bed when

Shawnee had seen her? No way. Denial was the only option left. "There's no girl in my bed," he growled.

Shawnee crowed with a quick laugh. "Ha! Don't try to lie, Kammie. Save it for your courtroom buddies. I can see right through it. I always could." She gave his arm a hasty, affectionate squeeze, and then she was off down the stairs, striding toward her car.

Kam turned slowly. Shawnee was gone, but that was the least of his worries. Now he had to deal with Ashley.

Ashley sat on the bed where Shawnee had left her, trying to get her act together. It was about time she attempted to get a little organization into her plans. Not to mention a little reality. The more she looked around herself and analyzed her situation, the more she realized she'd done something pretty darn silly.

Why couldn't she have done things the normal way? Why hadn't she just handed Wesley back his ring and walked away? If she'd done that, she'd have been on a plane, headed for the mainland by now. She'd have been free. It would all have been over.

Or... She shivered as she thought of it. If she'd stuck around, just the opposite might have happened. Wesley might have shouted, and her mother might have cried, and her father might have given her the benefit of one of his long, soul-searching talks, and she might have gone ahead and married the guy. Yes, that was more likely. And that was exactly why she'd known she had to run.

Still, things were pretty awkward. She was on her own, no direction known, with nothing, not even clothes on her back. She'd talked blithely to Shawnee about buying new clothes in a boutique, but then she'd realized she didn't have any money.

It was weird to have to think about money. She'd never had to think about money. It had always been there when she'd needed it. And she'd always had credit cards as a backup. But she hadn't brought her purse when she'd made her dash for freedom. Purses just didn't go with wedding gowns. It was generally assumed the bride would be taken care of and wouldn't need cab fare.

So, what was she going to do? Get a job as a waitress?

"They're gone." Kam was standing in the doorway. "You can come out, now."

It was the first time she'd really seen him in full light, and what she saw surprised her. She'd known he was handsome, but the morning sun revealed something more than ordinary good looks. His face was hard with lines that looked almost bitter, but his eyes were full of mystery and his mouth looked soft and sensual. His wide shoulders were tanned and defined with hard flesh that looked strong and just a little scary. She glanced at his bare chest, at the way his pajamas hung low on his hips, then looked away quickly, meeting his eyes and feeling herself coloring, though she silently cursed the fair skin that revealed it.

"Okay," she said, feeling as though her mouth were full of mush.

"Shawnee left you these." He was holding a pile of clothes, which he casually tossed onto the bed.

Grateful for something else to concentrate on, she picked up a brightly colored piece of cotton. "A sundress," she noted. Not quite her style, or her size, but it would certainly be better than the shirt. "Great. Now I can get dressed."

"Just a minute." He sat down on the edge of the bed, careful not to get close enough to touch her. He'd seen her reaction to his partially clothed state and he was bound and determined he wasn't going to follow her lead.

It was only natural, of course. They were two human beings. Physical attraction could happen to people who hated each other. No big deal. He was ready to ignore it if she was.

Glancing over, he couldn't help but notice the smooth, tanned skin of her legs. She looked small and young and defenseless—until he looked into her eyes. There was something ancient as the seas in those eyes. He wondered if it were wisdom or some trick of the light. Probably the latter. Things were seldom as good as they seemed.

"I take it you met my sister."

Ashley nodded.

"What did she say?"

Ashley thought for a moment. "Not much. She mostly listened while I stumbled through an explanation of what the heck I was doing here." She glanced up at him and grinned. She had her self-possession back and was feeling confident again. "Then she offered me a job at her café."

"She what?" He gaped at her in horror. "You didn't take her up on it, did you?"

Ashley paused before answering, considering. He seemed awfully anxious to make sure she didn't form any ties with people in his life, didn't he?

"I told her I'd think about it," she said, watching his eyes and seeing exactly what she'd expected—a quick flash of annoyance.

He started to say something and then thought better of it. Rising, he turned toward the dresser and pulled out a shirt and jeans, tucking them under his arm. "Why don't you go on and get dressed?" he said, his eyes fathomless as he looked back at her.

"Then come on out to the kitchen. There are doughnuts."

He disappeared through the doorway and she made a face at his vanishing back. "'There are doughnuts,'" she repeated mockingly, her voice only loud enough to be heard by herself. "If you're a very good girl, I may let you watch me eat one."

He was a very aggravating man. He didn't want her here, and she was going to oblige him by leaving as soon as she thought of someplace else to go.

That was the problem. Where the heck was she going to go? When she'd walked out the day before she'd had some vague idea of letting things settle down for a day or two and then showing up at her mother's hotel room, picking up her things and heading for the mainland. She supposed she was going to have to face Wesley at some point. Much as she dreaded it, it was only fair. But that whole plan had been founded upon the idea of staying here in what she thought was going to be an empty house. Now the house was only too full. So there went another ill-conceived scheme.

Now what?

Four

―――

The little blue sundress was too short at the hem and too big in the waist, but it hardly mattered. At least it covered what had to be covered. She ran a hand through her wiry hair, gave up on it, and headed for the kitchen.

Kam was sitting in the breakfast nook, looking dark and brooding. He'd changed into designer jeans and a white polo shirt that emphasized his tanned skin. She noticed once again that he was awfully attractive.

But that was neither here nor there. She wasn't looking for a boyfriend, just a port in the storm. It would be best if she kept that in mind. Flopping down across from him, she gave out her sunniest smile.

"Where are the doughnuts you advertised?" she asked, glancing at the crumbs littering an empty table.

A look of guilt crossed his face in an instant. "Oh. Sorry. I ate them."

"That was quick."

He swallowed and cleared his throat. "Actually, Shawnee—my sister—took most of them away. There was only one left and I just sort of gobbled it down without thinking."

"Ahh." She smiled again. "Is that your nervous habit?"

He frowned, displeased with the idea. "No. I don't have any nervous habit."

Her eyes widened dramatically. "Of course not," she said, her tone only slightly sarcastic. The look of wary distrust was still in his face. She wondered what exactly he was thinking. She had a feeling she knew at least part of it.

He was still confused over finding her in his bed this morning. He thought she was on the make, didn't he? He was afraid she might jump him at any moment.

This was too much. She supposed it was only natural that a man this good-looking and successful would have an ego to match, but that didn't make it any easier to take.

"Look, there's something we'd better get straight," she said evenly, pushing her hair back with an impatient gesture. "When I crawled into bed with you last night, I wasn't making a play for your bod."

He looked startled. Obviously he hadn't expected a direct explanation. But then, he was a lawyer, wasn't he? And they did tend to beat around the bush.

"I didn't say you were," he said defensively, his green gaze flickering over her and away again.

She smiled. "No, but you thought it."

His eyes darkened and his head went back. "You can read my mind, can you?" His tone was cool, almost cold. It was evident he didn't like this idea, either.

Her smile broadened. "You bet I can," she said, laying on the confident act, knowing it would annoy him. "And in doing so, I can see that you still don't believe me. You can't understand a woman needing something other than sexual comfort from a man, can you?"

Anger darkened his face like the sudden coming of a thunderstorm and his hard green eyes had her pinned to the wall.

"Listen, Ashley," he said, his words clipped and cutting. "I haven't accused you of a damn thing, and I would appreciate it if you would return the favor."

She nodded slowly. "You're right," she said, though her lips were thin. "Of course, you're right. I'm sorry." She sighed and leaned back in the seat. "In order to make it up to you, I'll try to explain."

His shoulders moved impatiently. "You don't have to explain anything."

"Yes, I do. I have to explain last night and why you found me next to you this morning."

He made a gesture of exasperation, but his words were moderate when he spoke. "Okay. Get it over with. Why did you come into my bed?" And then he locked her into his hard gaze, practically daring her to come up with a decent story.

She licked her lips and tried to find the right words to make him understand something that was more visceral than cerebral. "I needed human contact," she said at last, making it as simple as she could. "Haven't you ever felt like that? It was just such a weird night for me. There in the dark, after all that had happened to me yesterday, it all came crashing in. I just plain needed to feel a human nearby, to hear breathing, to feel warmth."

It all sounded so cut and dried here in the morning sunlight. During the night it had been a cry from her soul. But there was no way she could express that to him.

"Do you understand now?" she asked him, her blue eyes full of the need for his positive response.

He hesitated. He saw her need, but he wasn't going to lie to fulfill it. "I'm not sure that I do understand," he said slowly. "I still don't really know what you wanted."

"What I wanted?" She sat back and stared at him. At least he was honest enough not to push this off and pretend to be done with it. If he were going to be that honest, she had to try harder to fill in the blanks.

She closed her eyes and thought for a moment. "Remember that song Eliza Doolittle sings in *My Fair Lady?* About wanting a room somewhere?"

He remembered. He happened to be something of a fan of musicals of that era. But that didn't help much.

"Oh, come on," he scoffed after he'd thought about it for a moment. But actually, he just wanted to change the subject. He was ready to move on. Why was she telling him this? He didn't want to hear it. It was much too personal for him. He certainly wasn't going to do anything to help her with her problems. So why did he have to hear about them?

"Poor little rich girl," he said dismissively. "You most certainly have had a warm room whenever you've wanted one, and any number of enormous chairs."

She shook her head, wincing. "But that's not it. The song isn't just about being comfortable with material things. It's about being somewhere one belongs. Being a part of something of your very own. Like…like a family."

"A family?"

She could see the recoil in his face, and that explained a lot in one quick picture. Now he was afraid she was going to try to lasso him with a wedding ring. The man was paranoid. She wanted to laugh out loud.

"I never got that out of that song," he said, suddenly avoiding her eyes.

"Of course you didn't," she said crisply. "Because you're a man and a meanie and you don't want a family."

"A meanie?"

Their gazes met and held and suddenly they were almost laughing together at the incongruity of it all, but he looked away before it could happen.

"You seem to think you know a lot about me," he said dryly. "I wonder why."

"It's one of those feminine intuition things," she said, waving her hand. "Pay it no mind." She was ready to be done with this now, too. She'd explained as well as she could. If he still didn't get it, that was just too bad.

Sliding out of the seat, she went to the refrigerator. "Well, since you ate all the doughnuts, I'm going to have to scavenge for my breakfast, aren't I?"

"There's a ripe mango in the bowl on the counter," he told her.

"Really?" Turning, she picked up the bright orange fruit and turned it in her hand. "Are these really good? How do you eat them?"

"Get a knife out of the drawer," he advised. "Peel off the skin and cut off slices, or just take bites. But eat over the sink. It's pretty juicy."

It was extremely juicy, and before long she had mango juice dribbling down her chin and all over her arms. Kam jumped up and helped her with a clean towel, and then they were laughing together as he cleaned her up.

But only for a moment. He didn't seem to want to have a good time with her. He slid back into the breakfast nook while she finished cleaning the sink, as much to get away from her as anything else. At least, that was the way it looked to her. But she continued cleaning, ignoring him, thinking her own thoughts.

Meanwhile he watched her and, for the first time, he really looked at her. She was pretty in a mischievous sort of way. She looked like the grown-up version of little girls with twinkles in their eyes and freckles on their noses. Her eyes were sleepy and her hair was wild around her face, but he could see evidence of her background. He couldn't miss the patrician set of the jaw or the cool, noblesse oblige gaze her eyes took on at times. He should have picked up the hints right away when she'd said she was set to marry Wesley. She was from the same strata of society he moved in. Of course she was. He couldn't imagine dear old Wesley marrying anyone else.

There was no doubt about it. She was a spoiled little rich girl who had decided to play a wicked game on her fiancé. She'd gone and done a wild and crazy thing the day before. No doubt this was all a fun game of hide-and-seek, and she was waiting for Wesley to find her. He'd take bets that she lived most of her life on the edge of these melodramatic situations. He had to get her out of here as soon as possible. Melodrama did not mesh well with his life-style.

"So... what are your plans?" he said briskly.

"Plans?" She turned and looked at him, her face blank.

"Yes, those things we make to help guide our lives. Plans. You know, first I'll do this, and then I'll do that. That sort of thing."

She came over and slid into the seat across from his. Now he was being sarcastic. But why not? She supposed turnabout was fair play. "I know what plans are," she told him tartly.

"Do you?" He cocked an eyebrow. "I was beginning to wonder."

She shrugged. "I just don't have any, that's all."

His mouth hardened. "Surely you must have had something in your head when you walked out of that church and headed for my place."

He made it sound like she was a silly little brainless wonder. She knew that was exactly his purpose, but she wasn't sure why he was trying to keep her in that category in his mind. Did that help him keep his distance? Because, now that she thought about it, she realized that was what he had been doing all along.

"Yes," she said slowly, searching his eyes for clues as she talked. "In fact, I did have a plan of sorts. I intended to stay here in this house until I felt I was ready to leave."

"Here? Why here?"

"Because I'd been walking up and down your beach all week, and I noticed no one was living here. The place looks so nice from the beach side, with the geraniums blooming and the moss growing under the trees. The back window didn't look securely closed, and I thought I could get it open and climb in. Which is exactly what I did."

"So you cold-bloodedly picked this house—"

She grinned, cutting him off. "I *wisely* picked this house. I then had the bad luck to have the owner pick the same day to return to his vacation place. That was something I couldn't foresee, nor could I forestall."

"If I hadn't come back you would have been quite happily living in my house right now."

"Sure." She glanced around the neat little kitchen. "But I wouldn't be doing any damage."

"We'll never know that for sure," he said softly.

She looked at him quickly, surprised by his words and tone, but he was rising from his seat and she couldn't see his eyes.

"Well, you're here now," he muttered with his back to her. "You might as well stay until you're ready to go back."

He left the room and she stayed seated, staring after him. This was what she had wanted, a place to stay, a safe haven until she had herself back together and ready to return home to the mainland. Why wasn't she feeling happy and grateful?

There was something in the way he'd said it, something in the phrase "ready to go back" that bothered her. What did he think she was going back to? What did he think she was doing here in the first place? Rising slowly, she followed him.

He was just finishing up making the bed when she entered the room. It was too late for her to help with that, but she went straight to the chair and began folding the sheet and comforter she'd used the night before.

"I want to stay out of your way," she said in a chatty voice. "I know you came here to unwind from your work in Honolulu, and I don't want to do anything to keep you from doing that. So let me know what your day is going to be like, and I'll make it my business to avoid you."

"Don't worry about it," he said evenly. "I'll run when I see you coming."

The wry edge in his tone put her back up. After all, she was trying to be nice and accommodating. He didn't have to be insulting. She whirled to face him, and at the same time, he rose from tucking in the last corner of his bed, turning too quickly, and they collided. Nearly knocked off her feet, Ashley grabbed two handfuls of his shirt to keep from falling. At the same time, he reached to catch her and his hand clamped firmly on her breast.

"Oh!" she gasped, jerking away. But she didn't step back. Instead, she stared up at him, her blue eyes filled with surprise at the sensation he'd set off in her.

He scowled, furious. "Don't do that," he growled, cursing silently that anything had happened at all. But he hadn't done it on purpose, and she was surely overreacting with the gasp and look of wonder.

"Do what?" she asked, blinking, slightly stunned. Her breast was tingling and she wanted to put her hand over it, to stop it somehow. "*You're* the one who touched *me,*" Ashley reminded him.

Kam knew that. But she was the one who was making a big deal out of it. He should have moved away by now, but he was still standing there, much too close to her. Somehow he couldn't move, as though she held him in some sort of magnetic field. "I didn't mean to," he said clearly, staring down at her.

"Didn't you?" Her chin rose and she gazed at him challengingly. She knew very well he hadn't meant to touch her, but she was beyond reality now.

"No." His green eyes were glittering and his hands were balled into fists. "When I mean to touch a woman, I do it straight out. I don't play games."

She glanced at his luscious mouth and felt a quivering inside. "You're so sure of yourself," she said, a dare in her voice.

His lids drooped over eyes that had the luster of emeralds. "Damn right," he said softly.

Excitement skittered up and down her spine, setting every nerve ending on fire. She didn't stop to analyze what was going on here, because she knew that if she did that, she would have to make it stop. And some perverse imp inside her wouldn't let her do that.

Not now. Not when the tension between the two of them was so delicious.

She'd never felt this way with a man before, not this shimmering intensity. She was on a tightrope above a crevice, and there was no safety net.

"I don't think so," she said to him, confronting his arrogance with some of her own. Her eyes narrowed. "I think it's all a front."

That seemed to stump him. "What do you mean?" he demanded.

She knew she should be moving away, but instead she moved closer, as though daring him to do something about it. Now they were only inches apart.

"I don't think you touch women at all," she said in a mocking way meant to goad him. She knew she was playing with fire, but she couldn't stop. "I don't think you even like women very much."

There was a smoldering in his eyes now. He knew this was coercion of the most obvious sort. If he went any further with this, he would just be rising to her bait. He knew he should laugh and walk away. But for some reason he would spend the rest of the day trying without success to decipher, he didn't do it.

"I like women just fine," he said through gritted teeth. He moved deliberately, his hands firmly grasping her shoulders. He stared down into her eyes, and he knew he was going to kiss her.

"It's ditzy little spoiled rich girls I can't stand," he insisted, trying to convince himself as much as her.

"Why?" she taunted. "Can't compete?" She leaned forward slightly, lifting her face to his. "Or are you just scared you're not in my league?"

His fingers tightened on her shoulders and he drew her to him. His mouth was hard and hot and angry, and she opened to it like a flower to a sunny day. His heat filled her and she felt herself melt as it seeped into every nook and cranny. He was kissing her as she'd never been kissed before, setting off an excitement in her blood, something close to the thrill of a roller coaster ride.

She was used to polite kisses, subdued passion, desire that had more to do with recreation than ardor. This was different. There was something raw here. It stunned her, scared her, seared her with the certainty that she would need to have more, and very soon.

And then he was backing away, staring at her, wiping his mouth with the back of his hand, his eyes dark.

"I can't believe I fell for that," he murmured.

She smiled. A lovely feeling of lethargy was making her move in slow motion. "I can't believe I made you," she murmured back.

He opened his mouth to say something, but then stopped, thinking better of it. This was exactly what he didn't want to happen. Having a woman in the house was bad enough. If they were going to start doing this sort of thing, it would become impossible. He wasn't going to get close to another woman, not ever. He had to nip this in the bud.

Watching him, Ashley suddenly realized Kam's eyes were dark with trouble. This had really bothered him, and she didn't have a clue why that might be. She wanted to reach out and touch his arm, to comfort him, to tell him it was okay, the kiss really didn't mean a thing.

Because it really didn't. It had just been one of those things—one of those sweet, unavoidable things. Even now her heart beat a little faster as she thought of it. But it didn't mean a thing.

"You take life so seriously," she commented softly, her eyes suddenly misting a bit as she examined him. "Forget about it. It was nothing."

"Nothing?" His eyes were glittering again, and his brows were drawn together, completely rejecting her sympathy. "Like your almost-wedding was nothing, I suppose?" he drawled. "One day you're one step away from the altar with one man, the next day you're coming on to another. Is that what you mean by not taking life so seriously?"

Anger flushed her cheeks and she drew back, hurt and defensive. "I did *not* come on to you. It was just a simple kiss, mister. Don't make a federal case out of it."

His head went back and his eyes darkened. "Don't do it again."

She gaped at him. How dare he?

"I'll do it whenever I please, with whomever I please, thank you very much." She could read the condemnation in his eyes and that made her even angrier. "You just go worry about someone else's virtue. I'll take care of myself."

He shrugged as though her future was nothing to him. "I'm sure you will," he said dryly.

Turning, he almost stumbled over the wedding gown still hugging the floor. Leaning down, he picked it up by one lacy sleeve. "I suppose you'd better hang this up," he said, glancing at her. "I'm sure you'll want to use it later."

"Later?" She frowned. "I doubt it. I've sworn off men altogether."

Her anger cooled quickly. It always did. She gave a half shrug and tried to smile. "Sort of like you have with women. Maybe you could give me a few pointers later on—how to alienate the opposite sex in a few easy lessons. I could use them."

His hard glance was cynical as he slung the dress over the back of a chair. "It's just a matter of time. You'll go back."

That stopped her in her tracks. Had she really heard what she thought she'd heard? "I'll what?" she demanded, staring at him, eyes wide.

His mouth twisted. "Come on, you know you're going back. He's perfect for you—rich, smart—"

"Arrogant, bossy, intrusive. Sure, I just love obnoxious men."

He frowned. "But didn't you know all that before you agreed to marry him?"

She sank down onto the bed, feet dangling over the side. "No, to tell you the truth, I really didn't. Every time I saw him on the mainland, he was a perfect gentleman. When he came to visit us in La Jolla, we would have a ball."

She smiled, remembering. "We swam and went sailing and played billiards and went dancing until dawn. He was a different person from the man I found myself engaged to here in Hawaii."

Kam leaned back against the doorjamb, arms folded across his chest. "So what you're telling me is, you don't love him."

He said it as though he'd found the flaw in her argument, but she had no problem with the accusation. "I never loved him," she said loud and clear.

It was his turn to stare at her in surprise. "Then why were you going to marry him?"

Oh, brother. Didn't he understand anything? "Because I was unmarried and over thirty."

His face relaxed. Now he thought he understood. "Why, you crafty little conniver."

No, he just didn't get it. She sighed. "That's not it," she protested. "Try to think feelings rather than logical motivations. Don't you see? I'm not a conniver, at all."

"Not much. You were just after his money. Right?"

"Wrong." She laughed shortly. More money was the last thing she cared about. "You still don't understand."

What was the use? He was going to believe what he wanted to anyway. But she supposed she should at least try to get through to him.

"I just felt it was time. The nesting instinct was taking over. The signs were right. I wanted a family and..." Her voice trailed off and she shrugged helplessly.

He stared at her, unsure just what to believe. It was all so illogical the way she explained it. If she wasn't marrying Wesley for his money, what did she really want with a man she didn't love? He thought women were supposed to be the romantic ones, and yet here she was talking about nesting instincts and signs being right. There had to be a key to this whole thing that he was missing. He groped for it, but it just wasn't there.

"Haven't you ever been in love?" he asked her at last.

She hesitated for a moment, surprised by the question. Then she shook her head. "No," she said softly, searching his eyes. "I don't think so. Have you?"

That cloud came into his gaze again. "We're not talking about me. We're talking about you." He frowned, studying her intently. "Are you serious? You've really never been in love?"

She nodded. She'd never admitted this to anyone before. She'd decided that she was incapable of love. Surely if it were ever meant to happen it would have happened by now.

She liked people just fine, and she had always had lots of friends of both sexes. She enjoyed people, had a lot of fun. But there had never been that special feeling one read about in books or saw portrayed in the movies. Her heart strings had never gone "zing" and, though she'd listened hard, she'd never heard those bells on the hills.

She felt a vague sense of regret that she'd missed all that, but she didn't dwell on it much. After all, how could she pine away for something she'd never really known? And besides, she had about convinced herself that her life was much calmer and less chaotic without that love stuff. That is, until she ran from her own wedding. Would things ever be calm for her again?

"I've never been in love," she admitted to him without hesitation. "So I thought I might as well go for compatibility." Her laugh was rueful. "Only I messed up there, too. I really thought Wesley and I were perfect for each other. We went to the same schools, had the same sorts of friends, had families who'd known each other forever. I figured it was a perfect match."

His eyes were clouded and unreadable. "Sounds reasonable to me."

"Ah, but you see, I was dealing with insufficient data. Input determines output. If I'd only known then what I know now." She waved a hand in the air.

He made a sound low in his throat, something between a growl and a grunt, and at the same time he pushed himself away from the doorjamb.

"Cut the act, Ashley," Kam said scornfully. "You've been playing games since you ran from that church. I'm sure you've got everyone in a wonderful uproar, Wesley included. Don't you think it's time to go back and reap your reward?"

She stared at him, not sure, at first, what he could possibly be talking about. "My reward?" she asked blankly.

"Sure. The commotion you planned all this around." His smile was twisted with contempt. "You'll be the center of attention now, I can guarantee it. They'll be falling all over themselves to please you, Wesley included."

Well, that did it. It seemed incredible to her that anyone could have known her for more than twelve hours now and think such things of her. He'd been gruff and unfriendly since the moment they'd met, and now she had to face the fact that he was obviously determined to think badly of her no matter what evidence she presented.

She wasn't going to be able to stay after all. She'd been hoping to hang around for another day or two, but no, not in the face of this. Her self-respect demanded she get out right away.

"That's it," she said flatly, rising from the bed and tossing her wild hair back over her shoulder. "I'm going." She brushed past him and started for the front door.

"Oh, hold on." He didn't believe her. She could see it in his eyes. He thought she was still playing games.

"I'm out of here," she insisted, turning at the door to look back at him, her eyes burning with anger. "You can take that self-satisfied smirk off your face and go bury it in the yard. It belongs to another age, another time, my dear. Goodbye."

Opening the front door, she stepped onto the porch.

He followed her, still grinning, shaking his head as though he thought she was going to turn around any moment and come running back.

"What are you going to do?" he asked her, one eyebrow raised. "Do you have any money?"

She tossed her head. "I don't need money," she lied bravely.

His derisive laugh was all she needed to spur her on. "You don't have any money. You don't have any place to go."

She glared at him. She'd never been so angry. "Don't worry about me, mister. I've got resources."

He threw up his hands. "Where? What sort of resources?"

"They're all up here," she said, tapping her forehead with her finger.

He grinned again. "Yeah, I'll bet."

She knew what he was thinking. Well, let him think it. "I can get by on my wits," she informed him tartly. "I don't need you to pull me through."

He shook his head, trying not to grin anymore, but not succeeding very well. "Come off it, Ashley. You'd better stay here until you're ready to go back. A woman like you—"

"A woman like me?" Everything he said was just making matters worse. She threw out her arms and challenged him. "What do you know about me? You make assumptions and run with them. Great lawyer you must be."

Whirling, she continued her exit scene.

Kam watched as she walked out of his yard and down toward the sandy beach. The sunshine caught her hair and held it. She almost glowed.

He wanted to go after her, stop her, bring her back. He knew she didn't have any money. What the hell was she going to do? Live on the beach?

No, of course not. She knew a few people who could help her. A few very rich people. She would be okay. He was better off without her.

"Good riddance," he said aloud, so firmly that he almost convinced himself. He was free. He could go inside and make a pitcher of lemonade and take it out on the beach and sit back, absorb the sun, and let every nerve unwind. That was what he'd come for, and that was what he would do.

Whistling, he went to the refrigerator and opened the door, only to remember he hadn't brought along any lemons. So much for the lemonade. Beer would have to take its place.

He reached for the can of beer, lost his grip and dropped it on the same toe he'd stubbed that morning. Cursing violently, he hopped on one foot until the pain abated. Now he really needed that drink.

Glowering, he bent and picked up the can and popped the key. Cold foam shot out and soaked his face, hanging from his eyebrows, dripping from his hair.

"This is not my day," he muttered to himself, shaking off the beer and letting the drops fall where they might. In fact, it had been a long time since he'd had a day he liked.

But at least he was alone. That was all he really wanted.

Five

———

Ashley marched along the dirt road and thought of bad names to call Kam. Once she'd made it through the *p*'s, she felt better. But she was still angry with him. Imagine the nerve of the guy!

There had been an imperiousness to his tone, a certain lack of respect that had stunned her. She'd been accused of being a lightweight all her life, but she'd never been charged with being a manipulative little beast, until now.

But as she mulled it over, she realized it wasn't really surprising. After all, what had he seen of her? He'd seen her break into his house; he'd seen her shivering and crying in the night; and he'd found her snuggled into his bed without an invitation. And he knew she'd run away from her own wedding without confronting the situation as she should have. As far as he was concerned, she was a silly little impetuous fool in tattered clothing. Why should he give her any more respect than he might any bimbo off the street?

"Because I'm me, damn it," she muttered, and the anger coursed in her veins again. He had no right to talk to her that way, and even more, he had no right to think of her that way. She wasn't going to stand for it.

But what the heck was she going to do now? It had been all very well to tell Kam she could live by her wits in a strange place when she had no money, but she didn't have a clue as to how one did that.

Still, it had sounded good, hadn't it? She had to smile, remembering the look on his face when he'd realized she really was leaving. That look had been worth everything.

Well, almost everything. She was still left with a big void where a plan should be. What was she going to do?

She'd turned in from the beach and climbed an incline toward the part of the coast she knew best, the area she'd run from originally. The crest of the hill brought her to a fork in the road. Down one side was a winding path that led to a private entrance to the King's Way Country Club and Resort, where her mother and father were staying. Separately, of course, and with their respective new loves. She'd had dinner there just three nights before, with Wesley, and she knew his family were members. She would be on familiar territory. The man at the entry would allow her to use the house phone to call her mother, or her father, or Wesley, and this whole little escapade would be over. She would be back in the lap of luxury, the sort of good life she was used to.

She stared at the beautifully manicured lawns and the neatly laid out tennis courts and was tempted. It would be so easy. One little phone call.

But that would make this whole adventure she'd set off on look like the ridiculous prank Kam thought it was, wouldn't it? She would be like a child who'd put a knapsack over her back and run away from home, only to come back in the evening when hunger pangs began to strike. She would feel like an idiot. She couldn't do that. There was just no way.

Turning, she looked down at the other road. It led back down toward the ocean and right into the shabby little beachfront town with its tacky shops and dilapidated bar and grill and garish fast-food shacks. She hadn't been there before. Wesley and his family didn't patronize the area. They did their shopping inland at the major new mall with all its name stores. The beachfront town was for vacationers on a budget. What could she possibly find there?

There was no telling. But she would soon find out.

Kam's day had not improved with the coming of afternoon. His beach had been infested by noisy neighborhood children all day, making resting out there impossible. The book he'd brought to read turned out to be a political polemic and his radio was out of batteries. No sooner had he unplugged the stopped-up bathtub drain than the garbage disposal had stopped cold because of the mango skins Ashley had jammed down it.

He was beginning to wonder why they called this a vacation when it ended up being more work than ordinary life. He was just mulling that thought over when the front door opened and he swung around, expecting, beyond all logic, to see Ashley, and instead found his sister Shawnee sailing in as though she owned the place.

"Don't you ever knock?" he asked.

"I'm family," she said, looking startled. "If you want, I'll call out as I come in."

"Why not call ahead and warn me you're coming?" he grumbled, but actually, he wasn't sorry to see her. It had become awfully lonely in the past hour or so.

"Where is she?" Shawnee asked next, looking right and left as though Ashley might be hiding somewhere.

"Who?" Kam responded, though he knew full well.

She swung around and pinned him with a stern glance. "That young lady you were entertaining in your bed this morning."

He grimaced, refusing to fall for it. "She's gone," he said grimly, turning away.

"Gone?"

He nodded, sinking down to sit on the couch.

Shawnee dropped into the chair opposite. "What did you let her get away for?" she demanded.

He glared at his sister, not about to discuss this with her if he could help it. "I didn't want her."

"Oh." Her look was nothing if not skeptical on that count, but she held back a comment for now. "Where did she come from, anyway?" she asked instead.

Kam grimaced and leaned back, wondering where to begin. The beginning was probably about right. After all, she was gone now. What would it hurt to tell the truth?

"She broke into my house last night," he said calmly. "She came in through the back window."

"What?" Shawnee sat up and stared. She hadn't expected this. "Was she trying to rob you?"

"No. She just wanted a place to stay." He glanced at Shawnee, then away. In for a penny, in for a pound, he muttered to himself, and then aloud, "You see, she was running away from her wedding."

"Oh." Shawnee thought about that for a moment, biting her lip. "Was this before or after she'd said 'I do'?"

Kam had to smile at that one. "Before. Or so she says." He grinned. "Get this. She was going to marry Wesley Butler."

Shawnee slapped her thigh and laughed. "Hey, now I understand everything. I'd run away, too."

They chuckled together, both thinking of the Wesley they'd known all those years ago. Then Shawnee looked at her brother sharply.

"So... Where did she go?"

He shrugged, avoiding direct eye contact. That was the sore spot. He wished he knew. Just to set his mind at ease, of course. "I have no idea."

An answer like that was never going to satisfy Shawnee.

"Where do you think? What were her options? Whom did she know on the island? She told me she didn't have any money. You gave her some cash, didn't you?"

He swallowed and looked out the window. "No," he said defensively.

Shawnee gawked at him in horror. "You didn't give her any money? How do you expect her to make her way in a crazy touristy area like this without money?"

He put his hand through his hair in an impatient gesture. "Wake up, Shawnee," he said gruffly. "She went back to Wesley. She was only biding her time as it was."

Shawnee sat quietly for a long minute, studying her brother and thinking. Then, very slowly, she began to shake her head. "No," she said decisively. "The woman I met this morning did not go back to Wesley."

Kam frowned at her in surprise. He had known Shawnee all his life. She'd pretty much raised him and his two brothers, and he'd learned over the years to pay attention to her instincts. They usually turned out to be right on. Still, he couldn't help but think she was going way out on a limb on this one. "How could you possibly know that?"

She shrugged, her green eyes calm with knowledge. "I just know it. She's out there somewhere, trying to get by, with no money and no one to help her."

She glared at her brother. Sometimes she was afraid he was incapable of human warmth. She didn't want him to be a sensitive modern man exactly—knowing that was too far from the mark to ever become reality for Kam. But she had often wished she could make him feel a little more, think a little more about what others were thinking and feeling.

"How could you let her go like that?"

Annoyance flared in his gaze. "Shawnee, I hardly know her. She broke into my house. How much do you owe people who break in, anyway? Maybe I should have loaned her my car."

"Maybe you should have, you big lug." She chewed on her lip for a moment, frowning. "Look at it this way. You cast her out into the snow without a penny. What could she do but go back to Wesley? You pushed her back into his slimy arms."

Her eyes filled with tragedy. "Oh, Kam, how could you have? She's a nice girl. You should have done better by her."

He started to argue back, then thought better of it. After all, how long could he go on arguing about something neither of them knew anything about? Rising impatiently, he turned to look down at her.

"She's gone now, so all this is moot," he said crisply. "Give it up. It's over."

Shawnee leaned forward and stared at him accusingly. "You don't care?"

He threw out his arms in exasperation. "Why should I care? She means nothing to me."

"But I thought there was a little something between the two of you."

He began to pace, and a vein began to throb at his temple. "You thought wrong."

Shawnee sighed, shaking her head. "Kammie, Kammie, I'm about to give up on you," she wailed.

Leaning back, he turned his face to the sky. "Hallelujah!" he breathed.

"You say that now," Shawnee complained, frowning fretfully. "But if you don't watch out, you're going to end up like Cousin Reggie, sitting out on a cliff overlooking the ocean by the hour, waiting for the mermaid of your dreams to come popping out of the surf and take you in her arms."

Kam straightened, suddenly concerned. "Is he still doing that?"

She nodded. "Daily. He's gone completely over the edge. He won't talk to anyone, he'll hardly eat. He keeps babbling about his lost love and no one can get through to him. He doesn't want to hear about anything else. We don't know what to do about him."

"Leave him alone," Kam said softly, staring into space. "Just leave him alone."

Shawnee gazed at him, shaking her head. "First, Cousin Reggie, now this," she muttered to herself, gathering up her things and preparing to go. "Maybe there is a streak of insanity in the family, after all."

Kam said goodbye to his sister, but he hardly noticed her leaving. His mind was off on other things.

Shawnee's visit had put him in a foul mood. The day had been bad enough before, but now it was even worse. The sun wasn't hot enough. The beer wasn't cold enough. The ocean wasn't blue enough. He was dissatisfied with everything he looked at. He tried to read, but he couldn't concentrate. Wandering through his empty house, he spotted his reflection in a mirror and stopped to look at it for a moment.

What he saw hardly looked familiar. When had he lost that youthful roundness to his face? Where had those lines come from? His mind flashed back to a time a few years ago when he'd stood beside a young woman and they had both laughed, looking into a mirror very much like this one. He'd looked so much younger then. He'd been so much younger then. Ellen's death had aged him like nothing else in his life ever would again.

"You're going to have to go looking for her, aren't you?" he asked himself.

And the answer was clear. He wasn't going to be able to rest until he found Ashley. Either she was with Wesley, in which case he'd wash his hands of her. Or she was out there somewhere, trying to find shelter, and he would give her some cash to tide her over. Then maybe he could relax and find the peace he'd come here for.

He headed straight to the King's Way Country Club and Resort, never doubting for a moment that she had made a beeline for the place. It was her sort of establishment, after all. She would feel at home there. She might even know someone there who would help her. So he bought a visitor's pass at the entry kiosk and went in.

She wasn't in the bar. She wasn't in the restaurant. She wasn't even out on the tennis courts, although a lot of young, pretty women in short white skirts were, and he lingered to watch a few volleys. There wasn't a sign of Ashley anywhere, and when he asked a counter clerk if he'd seen her, Kam got a negative reply.

But what was he worried about? For all he knew, she was already back in Wesley's arms.

That was it. She'd gone back to Wesley, just as sure as the sun was headed into the sea, just as he'd predicted. Of course she had. He was making a fool of himself, wandering the streets, and she was back with Wesley, crying crocodile tears and promising never to worry him again.

That did it. Kam was going home. He was going to forget about Ashley and her problems. She could obviously take care of herself.

But once in his car, his attention was drawn to the little town, and he decided one run down along the beach wouldn't hurt. He cruised the shoreline, watching tourists strolling arm in arm, then parked and walked out into the strip of shops along the ocean front. Every blonde caught his eye, but not one of them was Ashley.

He walked back toward his car, avoiding a boy on a bicycle and turning when he heard a man shout nearby.

"Hey, Lennie," called a young fellow in a cheap suit, leaning out of the doorway of the bar and grill. "You gotta come see this. We got a little blonde in here, hustlin' pool. Come on. It's something else."

He stopped dead in his tracks, a shiver of vague foreboding chilling him as he watched the young man he assumed must be Lennie dash in through the doorway, his face eager. It couldn't be. No. She was blond, and she was little, but pool? No way. It couldn't be. Could it?

She had mentioned billiards, but there was a major leap from a gentlemanly game of billiards to hustling pool. There was just no way. He might as well go home and get on with his vacation.

Taking one last, sweeping look at the beach area, he turned and headed toward his car again.

The late-afternoon sun was blinding him, and suddenly the short ride home seemed too lonely. He didn't want to go back just yet. Turning, he scanned the little town and decided on the bar and grill. He might as well take a look and see this blond phenom who was hustling pool.

Cautiously, he entered the building and squinted in the dark, smoky atmosphere. The jukebox was playing a loud rock tune and raucous laughter filled the air. There was a burning smell over and above the cigarette smoke. Something was cooking on the grill, no doubt. The room was too hot, too loud, too smoky, and some sort of strange intensity seemed to vibrate in the mix.

The clientele was mostly male, it seemed, and the few women he saw were quietly gathered at far tables. The men were assembled around the center of the room, and he pushed his way through the crowd to see what the attraction was.

It was the blonde playing pool, of course. There she was, smacking balls with a brisk self-confidence, ignoring the provocative things men were calling out to her, focusing on her game and doing very well at it.

Kam watched, swallowing hard. It was exactly what he'd been afraid of. He was shocked to see Ashley holding a cue stick and calling out, "In the side pocket," before leaning forward and taking a shot that sent a ball spinning to its named destination without a waver.

It was a strange thing, but she seemed like a different person from the woman he'd found in his house the night before. She had the same wild hair, the same slight build, and she was wearing his sister's old sun-

dress. But there was an air about her, a flair, a strut
that was new.

She straightened and smiled as the crowd ap-
plauded. "That's game, gentlemen," she said, tossing her hair back with a triumphant gesture as a young
man stepped back, shaking his head. Reaching out,
she picked up the pile of greenbacks that had been
perched on the corner of the table and slipped them
into the pocket of her blue sundress.

"Who's next?" she asked brightly, surveying the
crowd.

There was a high flush on her cheeks, a sparkle in
her eyes. She looked like a woman on top of her game,
full of excitement, ready for anything. Despite all
that—and he had a lot of reservations about this situation—he had to grin as he watched her. She looked
great.

But his grin faded when he looked into the faces of
the men in the crowd. Most of them were ordinary
observers, but here and there he saw those who had
more than admiration in their eyes, more than
amusement. He could almost smell the danger.

"I'll go next," he said loud and clear, turning back.

Spinning, she gasped as she saw him, her eyes widening slightly. But she regained her composure and
smiled politely. "Be my guest. Would you like to
break?"

"Just your neck," he whispered as he passed her,
going for the cue rack just beyond the table. "What
the hell do you think you're doing here?"

"Taking care of myself," she whispered back.
Aloud she said, "You call it, mister. What are we
playing?"

"Russian roulette," he muttered, taking his place
beside her at the table. He caught her gaze with his
own and made sure she saw the challenge. "You must

feel lucky tonight," he said softly. "But even the best of luck runs out sometime."

"How about nine ball?" she suggested, ignoring his remarks.

She eyed him levelly, as though sizing him up as an opponent, and for the first time, he felt a tremor of unease. His plan was to beat her, then get her out of here. The key to success was going to be winning at this game.

He was pretty good at pool. He had a natural, fluid style that looked easy but had been developed over the years in law school. As he chalked up his cue, he looked at the flat, green felt playing field and then glanced at Ashley.

She was standing easily, not paying any attention to the catcalls from the audience. Her mind was on the game, and in the moment that he really saw that, he knew something important. She could beat him. It was written all over her.

That assessment was borne out as she played, leaning over the table, draping herself like a pretzel to get the best angle, ignoring the fact that the short sundress revealed a lot of leg as she did so. Her shots were firm and true, and they always went exactly as she called them. Every time. Like clockwork. Like a well-programmed robot.

She was beautiful, poetry in motion. She took charge as though she'd been born to play this game. He didn't stand a chance.

"Let me win," he murmured to her when she passed close by on her way to a particularly difficult shot.

Her eyes flashed at him. "Dream on," she snorted.

He grabbed her arm, staring down into her huge blue eyes. "The place is full of men, Ashley."

Her eyes sparkled. "I know. I've got them all in the palm of my hand." Pulling away, she took her shot and made it with ease.

He followed her, trying to make her understand. "This is not good, Ashley. They're with you right now. But they'll turn on you like a pack of wolves if you show any weakness."

She laughed at him, pushing him aside so that she could get to her next shot. "Oh, please, Kam," she said, patting his arm. "Spare me the melodramatics."

"Let the lady play, buddy," someone from the crowd yelled. And suddenly Kam realized that the one they turned on might be him.

He went back to concentrating on the game, and he played better than he'd ever played before, sinking impossible shots. But she was one step ahead of him at every turn. And on her, it looked so easy.

"Don't you ever make a mistake?" he asked her gloomily.

"Never," she said, throwing him a sunny smile that had a spark of mischievous intent. "Why don't you just bow to the inevitable and let someone else take a turn?"

Volunteers called out, but Kam shook his head. "No. I'm not beat yet," he growled, moving in to try yet again. "Stand back."

He went on doggedly. Meanwhile his mind was busy considering and discarding one desperate plan after another. How was he going to get her out of here if he couldn't beat her at pool? As long as she was winning, the crowd wouldn't let her leave—and he would have no excuse to compel her to. What the hell was he going to do?

It had been a bad day all around so he wasn't counting on any luck coming his way, but that was exactly what happened. In the back, behind the bar, someone dropped a whole tray of glasses just as Ashley took a shot.

It didn't faze her one bit. The ball still came straight and true toward its goal. But the crowd swung around like one large being, craning to see what had happened behind the bar, and in that moment of anonymity, Kam's hand shot out and covered the hole, taking a nasty rap as the ball hit his knuckles and ricocheted off.

"Hey!" Ashley cried out. "You cheated!"

"You missed," he retorted, eyes bright, and suddenly he was the one grinning.

The crowd was back, and most of them were groaning.

"Did you see that? She missed," said one tattooed muscle man mournfully, as disillusioned as though he'd just heard there really was no Santa Claus. "Ah, man. She missed."

"But...but..." Ashley looked at the crowd beseechingly, then turned and glared at Kam. "Tell them, Kam," she ordered. "Tell them why I missed."

"You missed because of the glasses breaking," he said with only slightly fractured honesty. "And that means, I win."

Turning, he put down his cue very carefully, then faced her. Her blue eyes were dark with fury. He grinned at her, then turned to the crowd with a grand flourish meant to get them behind him.

"And I didn't play for money," he said, projecting to the far corners of the room.

Ashley stared at him, frowning, but she was unprepared when he reached out and swung her up into his arms.

"Hey!" she cried out, rearing back.

"Play along, Ashley," he warned her firmly. "One way or another, I'm getting you out of here. Let's try to do it with a little dignity."

"Dignity!" she raged between clenched teeth. "Dignity for you, maybe. I get to feel like a sack of potatoes."

There were murmurings in the crowd. A few shouts. And nobody moved when he started toward them. The mood was not good. He'd hoped for better. If they didn't part and make way, he was going to have to shove his way through, and that wouldn't be easy carrying Ashley.

He approached, and still nobody moved.

"Mind making way?" he asked, nodding to a burly man in a ponytail. "She's heavier than she looks."

There was a moment of hesitation when fate hung in the air. Then the burly man laughed, and suddenly everyone was moving back, leaving him a path.

"Hey, you bring her on back tomorrow, okay?" one male voice rang out. "I didn't get a chance to show her my moves."

"We'll see," Kam called back into the sea of general laughter, saluting just before he turned away and escaped through the double doors.

The moment he was out of sight of the bar, he dropped her to her feet and grabbed her wrist to lead her.

"Come on," he said urgently. "Let's get out of here before they change their minds."

She ripped her hand away from his, but she came along beside him willingly enough, though not without some complaint.

"I can't believe they let me go with you like that," she cried, glaring at him as they hurried along. "What do they think I am, some piece of property to be handed around?"

His grin flashed white against his tan skin. "I won you fair and square," he said, knowing his words would infuriate her even further.

She whirled on him, completely outraged. "You did not! You cheated."

Grabbing her arm, he propelled her the last few feet to the car.

"Nevertheless," he told her firmly. "I won."

They had reached the car and he opened the passenger door, giving her a gentle shove to get her seated, then walked around to the driver's seat and started the engine.

"Where are we going?" she asked him. She was frowning, but the pout was slight and he was pretty sure it wasn't going to last. At this point, it was more for principle than passion.

"Just up the hill where we can talk," he reassured her, backing out of the parking space. "Hang on. We'll be there in a minute."

The view from the hill was spectacular. The ocean stretched out forever, blue and green and gray, with whitecaps where the wind caught the water and sent it high. The white sands of the beach, the green belt of jungle in between, made a brilliant contrast of colors and textures. Off to the left were the neatly clipped lawns and courts of the King's Way. To the right was the picturesque town. Kam pulled to the side of the dirt road and turned off the engine, slumping in his seat as he turned to look at Ashley.

"How have you survived for thirty years?" he said, looking her up and down.

He had to admit, she looked good. Beating all those men at pool seemed to have revived a certain color in her cheeks and sparkle in her eyes, something that hadn't been there earlier in the day. Still, living on the edge of danger could go either way. Didn't she know that?

"What do you mean?" she demanded indignantly. She was pretty darn proud of herself for what she'd done. "I was thrown out into the middle of unfamiliar territory, and I managed to find a way to survive on my own. You should be proud of me."

Proud of her! He wanted to wring her neck. But as he calmed down, he had to acknowledge, begrudgingly, that what she'd done was worthy of admiration—of a sort. Here he'd thought she was just a little bubble-headed rich girl who wouldn't be able to figure out how to use a public phone, much less make her way in the world on her own.

She'd done that, done it in spades. She was brave and resourceful—that much was all to the good.

What bothered him was her total lack of awareness of danger. Didn't she have any conception of what she was risking by her bold behavior?

"Didn't you see the way some of those men were looking at you?"

She blinked. Was that all? "Looks aren't going to hurt me."

He shook his head impatiently. "Looks can build to other things."

She shrugged. "They liked what they saw. Is that so terrible?" Her gaze sharpened as she searched his eyes. "Are you going to make a blanket condemnation of men now?" she asked, just the barest hint of a taunt in her voice. "You sound like some of those campus feminists. Do you really think that men can't control themselves? Do you think they're all insatiable beasts who pounce on every woman who passes their way?"

He groaned, leaning back. "I'm not saying that at all."

"Then, what are you saying?"

His mouth twisted. "In any large group of men, most of them are going to be great guys, but there are very often a few who feel it is their duty to revert to the call of the wild."

She knew he had a point, but she wasn't about to concede it to him. Instead she set her mouth primly. "You give people a lot of credit, don't you?"

"I do." He shook his head, trying to make her understand. "I think people are basically pretty good. And the best way to keep them that way is to watch them like hawks at all times."

She looked at him and had to hold back a giggle. "Whew. Some philosophy of life you've got there."

He had to restrain himself from shaking her. "All I'm asking you to do is think twice before you put yourself into a situation like that again. Okay?"

She hesitated, then smiled at him, and the effect was as though the sun had come up on fast forward.

"Aye-aye, sir," she said, saluting him with two fingers to her forehead.

"And anyway, where did you learn to play pool like that?"

"At school." She sighed. "In college, I was the local champ. I used to practice by the hour while I was busy flunking out of my chemistry major. That was before I switched to art and found my calling."

He looked at her, shaking his head. "You're quite something, aren't you?" he said softly.

Was that good or bad? She wasn't sure. "That depends on what you mean," she countered. She smiled at him, almost kittenish for a moment. Then the smile evaporated again.

"Anyway, now what?"

He had to steady himself. She shifted gears a little too quickly for him. He was still reacting to her smile. For some reason, it seemed to have sliced right down into his soul, and he needed time to recover his equilibrium.

"I don't know," he said at last, looking away from her and out to sea. "What do you want to do?"

She made a face. "Oh, I don't know," she said teasingly. "Climb Mt. Everest. Discover the cure for weight gain. Establish world peace. Maybe buy a new Jaguar." Cocking her head to the side, she smiled at him again. "Why? What do you want to do?"

He found himself smiling back, though it was surely against his nature. "Keep you out of trouble," he muttered.

"Me?" She had the gall to look surprised. "I'm never in trouble."

He let out a long sigh and leaned his head back, closing his eyes. "Maybe the events of the last twenty-four hours have somehow slipped your mind," he said, trying to keep the impatience out of his voice and not succeeding. "Or maybe your days are always like that."

"Well, now that you mention it…" She poked him with her foot. "It has been a little wild. But I'm getting tough. I can handle it."

He opened his eyes and gave her a long, sideways glance. "When are you planning to go back?" he asked quietly.

"What?" She stiffened. "Go back where?"

He turned and faced her fully. "You know where. You know you're going to have to—"

She made a gesture as though she were about to clap both hands over her ears so she wouldn't have to hear this. "Don't you get it?" she asked sharply. "I will never go back to Wesley."

He hesitated, then looked out at the ocean again. "Will you come back to me?" he asked so softly she hardly heard it.

"To you?" she repeated, staring at him.

He moved uncomfortably in his seat. "Well, I don't mean it quite that way." He glanced at her, then away again. "I just feel bad about some of the things I said to you this morning. Why don't you come on back? You could stay at my place until you're ready to move on."

She didn't answer for a long moment, and finally he had to turn and look at her. He found her waiting for exactly that. She didn't smile.

"Why should I come back?" she asked evenly. "I've got money now. I can stay anywhere I want." Her blue eyes searched his for his reaction.

He didn't give away anything. "That's right," he agreed. What else could he do?

"That's right," she echoed firmly. She wanted it clearly established that she was a free agent, not some clinging dependent.

He shrugged. "So, go already."

That was the hard part. "Where?"

"Well, that's the point, isn't it? You don't know anybody." His grin was twisted. "Except me."

She took a deep breath and shook her head. "If I come back and stay with you, you have to promise not to treat me like an alley cat."

"An alley cat." He frowned at her. "When did I ever treat you like an alley cat?"

Her gaze as it met his was cool and level. "This morning. Surely you remember. You acted like I was brainless and helpless and needed a keeper."

He swallowed and looked at his hands on the steering wheel. "I'm sorry I made you feel that way," he said stiffly. "That wasn't fair."

"No. It wasn't." Her smile was smug. "I guess I proved I could take care of myself."

He grimaced ruefully. "I guess you did," he agreed, though he had a hard time getting it out. "At least, up to a point. I don't know what you would have done if all those men—"

"All those men again!" She laughed. "You're really fixated on them, aren't you?" Her smile turned impish. "Why, Kam? Were you jealous?"

"Jealous?" He straightened in the seat, frowning fiercely. "What do I have to be jealous about? You're not my girl. You're Wesley's."

All her sunshine disappeared and the storm was back in her blue eyes. "I am not Wesley's. Will you stop saying that?" She took a deep breath and looked away. "It's over," she said evenly.

But he couldn't let her get away with that. "It won't be over until you see him again. You have to tell him face-to-face that it's over. Then it might be true."

She stared, floored for the moment by his logic. He was absolutely right. It was a good thing he kept throwing it up to her, because she was going to have to face it sooner or later.

"I can't do that yet," she said softly, avoiding his gaze. "I'm not ready. I need a little time."

"That's exactly why I think you should come back with me."

He glanced over at her down-turned face and had to restrain himself from reaching out to lift it with a finger under her chin. For just a moment, he had a surge of panic. He couldn't take her home with him. What the hell was he going to do with her? He was so concerned with her tilting at risky things, and now he was practically begging for danger himself.

She was too appealing. He knew that very well, and yet here he was, asking her to stay around. That wasn't like him, and he couldn't really understand why he was doing it now.

"Guilty, despite the insanity plea," he muttered to himself.

"What?" She looked up at him.

"Nothing." He clutched the steering wheel to keep from touching her. "Well, what's the verdict? Are you going to come with me? Because if not," he added hurriedly, "I do know a nice little cheap motel where you could stay. I could drive you there right now. If you want."

He waited, heart beating just a little too hard, for her answer.

She reached out slowly and laid her open hand on his arm. "Thanks, Kam," she said. "I'd like to go with you."

Something surged in his chest and that was when he knew he'd made a really big mistake. Ashley wasn't just coming to stay. Ashley was coming to change his life.

Six

The problem of where Ashley was going to sleep loomed between them like an uninvited guest who insisted on monopolizing the conversation at a dinner party. It was there from the moment they stepped into the house.

Ashley took a long bath right after they arrived back at the house, then put on the sundress again and went out to sit with Kam in the backyard, watching the sunset. They sat together on a wrought-iron bench beneath a protected arbor dripping with ginger and honeycomb and plumeria blossoms. Birds sang in the trees. Insects hummed. And the scent of the flowers spiced the atmosphere around them.

She was feeling lazy and languorous, almost at peace—for now. Kam had made a pitcher of light margaritas and they sipped together in companionable silence for a while.

A neighbor's black cat strayed into the yard and walked right up to Kam, leaping up into his lap and arching happily as Kam's big hand stroked it again and again. Ashley watched, interested in his gentleness in touching the animal, the tender way he spoke to it. For a man who was all gruffness and prickly most of the time, he seemed to have a sea change when the cat arrived.

"Why don't you like women?" she asked him suddenly, feeling relaxed and brave. "Who broke your heart?"

He looked at her as though she'd been spouting phrases from a lost language.

"Who said I don't like women?" he said.

She rolled her eyes at him. "You don't have to say it. You can't seem to help but act it."

He went back to petting the cat. "I like women just fine," he said dismissively, his tone abrupt. "You're barking up the wrong tree, lady."

A secretive smile flitted across her face. "So you're not going to tell me."

"Tell you what?" he responded, all phony innocence.

"Who broke your heart and why?"

He stared at her, his eyes luminous in the twilight. For a moment she was afraid she had made him angry again, but just when she was about to apologize, he said softly, "Her name was Ellen. And she didn't break my heart. She died."

"Oh." Now she really was sorry. She moved uncomfortably on the bench and looked at him with all sincerity. "How awful."

"It was a long time ago." The cat jumped off his lap and he watched it sashay slowly across the yard. "Are you a cat person or a dog person?" he asked quietly.

"What?" The sudden change in subjects was disconcerting. Her mind was still full of this Ellen person and how her death must have helped mold Kam into the reclusive sort of man he seemed to be. But she quickly realized he'd done it on purpose, and she supposed he had a right to do that if he wished. She was prying. But there were things she had to know.

"Oh. Cat, I guess. I've always had a cat or two in my life." She looked across at him. "How about you?"

"Neither," he said calmly. "I don't like being responsible for the well-being of any other entity."

She chortled, pulling her legs up under her and getting comfortable. "What a roundabout way to say you don't like pets," she noted. "See what happens when you go to law school. Do they make you practice talking like that?"

He allowed a slight smile to soften his face. "No. It just comes naturally, I guess."

She laughed aloud. "Did you talk that way when you were a kid?" She adopted a mocking tone of stilted speech. "'Mrs. Jones, as the party of the first part, I hold invalid your request for a homework assignment. My document was destroyed by excessive mastication on the part of my canine companion.'"

He couldn't help but grin at that. "I only wish I'd been that bright at an early age," he told her. "I spent my younger days wasting time at the beach, surfing, and at the movies, looking in on lives that were a lot more interesting than mine."

Aha! she thought to herself. More clues as to why this reserved, distant man is who he is.

"I was pretty much a beach bunny myself," she told him, swirling her finger through the salt on the rim of her glass. "Some summers I hardly even came in for a shower."

"Yeah, but you were a rich girl. You didn't need to make a living."

"Says who?" She straightened, indignant. "I graduated from college with a degree in art, I'll have you know. And I've been doing illustrations for children's books for the last ten years."

That surprised him. "I stand corrected."

She saluted him with her glass. "You stand with egg on your face, mister," she amended pointedly. "Things are not always as they seem. Or even as you assume."

He hid his smile behind his glass. "That's quite true. I'll have to be more careful in the future."

She grinned. "See that you are. And you could start by getting rid of the idea that I'm ever going back to Wesley."

He put down his glass on the little table in front of them and stared at it. There were still too many unanswered questions about that chapter. He'd started out thinking she was a flake who had run on a whim, and probably just to stir things up. But now he wasn't so sure. She surprised him every time he turned around. The better he got to know her, the more he was convinced there was a depth to her he hadn't noticed at first. Getting to the bottom of what had gone wrong with her engagement might help get to the bottom of what this woman was really all about. And for some strange reason, he had to know.

"What happened?" he asked at last. "What turned you against the poor guy?"

She leaned back and stared up at the stars, just barely beginning to emerge in the night sky. "I got to see him on his own turf, so to speak. And suddenly he was a completely different person."

He threw her a skeptical look. "You mean, he was a real sweetheart on the mainland?" he asked sardonically.

She considered, head to the side. "Well, not exactly. I mean, I knew he wasn't what you would call a sensitive nineties' sort of man. But then," she added with a quick smile, "neither are you."

He grunted to acknowledge her point. "But you still wanted to marry him."

"Oh, sure."

"Why?"

She giggled and turned to watch his face when she gave her answer. "Because he asked me."

His raised eyebrow was incredulous. "Are you trying to tell me no one else had ever asked you before?"

"No, no. I've had other offers." She sobered wistfully. "But none lately."

He stared at her, appalled. Sometimes he just couldn't figure women out. "So you thought you'd better snap Wesley up, just in case there really weren't any more offers coming down the pike."

Her smile didn't come quite so easily this time. "That just about covers it."

He grimaced. "That's still pretty cold-blooded," he said, looking as though he'd eaten something that didn't agree with him. "What kind of wife were you planning to be?"

She hesitated, wondering if she should really go into this with Kam. She wasn't in the habit of spilling her guts to all and sundry. But there was something about this silent, moody man that inspired confidence. Whatever else, he was honest in his reactions. He didn't pretend to agree when he didn't at all. He didn't tell her sugar-coated niceties to keep her happy. He called them as he saw them, and at the same time, he had a way of allowing her to have her own opinions, even if they were different from his.

She wasn't used to that. She came from people who held back the truth as long as possible, hoping to change it into something prettier, sweeter, easier to swallow. And at the same time, they didn't want to hear sounds from another quarter. Everything had to be just so.

Kam was different, and she liked that. It made her feel as though he valued her as a person. So she plowed ahead.

"Like I said, I was rather fond of him. I'd known him for years and years. I thought I knew him through and through. So I was planning to be quite a good wife to him."

She turned her face and looked at the sea, its silver sheen highlighting the black waves. "I didn't expect fireworks, but I did think we would get on well together. We might have children. I would get involved with the kids. He would play golf. Sometimes we might take trips together, Hong Kong, maybe, London."

She looked at him earnestly. "Don't you see? I really wanted it to work. I want a family. When a woman hits thirty, she knows the days are beginning to count, and she doesn't have an unlimited supply. It's not like I was desperate. It was more that I hadn't really fallen in love after fifteen years of trying, so I decided to settle for the next best thing. Do you see?"

He didn't answer. The sun had disappeared long ago, and she could hardly make out his features in the dark night that had flooded in around them. For some reason, she needed to make that connection, and she reached out and touched his arm.

"Do you see?" she repeated. She needed to know that he understood.

"Tell me why you changed your mind about him," he said calmly, and she drew back.

"Things started off all right," she said. "I flew in about two weeks ago. I fell in love with the island right away. The air is so soft here, you know? Everything comes in such lush colors. Everyone smiles. At first, I was just so happy to be here, I went around in a dream."

He nodded, though she couldn't see it. She was so different from the way he was. Where he liked to move on an even plane, not veering too wildly from one side to the other, she took off like a rocket and then sank back to earth with a thud. She was like Ellen that way. Very like Ellen. For a moment a chill went down his spine and he wished he hadn't asked her back.

"But then I began to notice something. The Wesley I thought I knew didn't seem to exist here. All of a sudden, I was engaged to marry a man who seemed like a real jerk. He sort of..." She crinkled her nose, thinking. "He sort of swaggers here, and orders people around in a way I never noticed before."

Kam laughed softly. "Yes, that is the Wesley we know and love."

"Well, I didn't love him in the first place, but once he started acting like that, I didn't even like him anymore. Now how was I supposed to put up with a man like that till death do us part?"

He studied what he could see of her in the dark. He could go in and turn on the outside light, but that would ruin this mood, and somehow he liked it. People opened up better in the dark, and Ashley was certainly opening up about this Wesley business. He was trying hard to understand, but he still wasn't sure he got it entirely.

"But if all that was so clear to you once you got here and looked around," he prodded, "why did you wait until the middle of the wedding to make your move?"

"I was going to stick it out. I figured I'd made my bed, and all that." She sighed, stretching her legs out in front of her. "But then my family arrived."

"Your family."

"Yes. My mother and her new boyfriend. Excuse the expression, but gag me with a spoon. I hate when she gets new boyfriends. Of course, I hate it even worse when she gets new husbands."

He frowned sympathetically. "Does she do that a lot?"

She nodded. "She's looking for the fourth one right now."

He shook his head, slightly amused, though he could tell these quests by her mother hurt her to some extent. "That does seem like more than her share," he said dryly.

"Tell me about it! And then there's my father. He showed up with his new girlfriend. I'm not sure if she has her high school diploma yet. Don't they have an age limitation on that? She can't be more than twelve."

"Ashley," he said, laughing.

"I'm serious," she said with a grin in her voice that belied her claim. "I think she's still wearing a training bra."

He laughed, but chided her. "Hey, come on. You're talking about your father."

"Okay. I'm sorry. I forgot you take everything so seriously. I didn't really mean it. Christina is twenty-four. She just acts twelve."

He shook his head. "So having your family around you wasn't a comfort?"

"Having my family around me was a pain in the neck. And it brought home to me how futile it all was. What I was trying to do, I mean."

"How so?"

"Well, look at the two of them—my dear parents. They've never made a commitment they've kept longer than six months. They haven't a clue on how to maintain a relationship with any sort of integrity. And here I am, the result of their first disastrous marriage. What made me think I could do any better than they did?"

He waited a moment, but she didn't continue. "That was it?" he said at last. "That was what convinced you to give up?"

She sighed and wondered if she should go on. But, what the heck? She'd gone this far. "That wasn't it, exactly, but it did set the stage. The thing that killed it all for me was when Wesley snuck into the bridal dressing room where I was getting ready for the wedding."

He swung around to look at her. "Do you mean to tell me you ran away from your wedding because the groom saw you before the vows? This is incredible. You can't mean it."

"I don't mean it." She frowned at him, puzzled. "Where did you get such a crazy idea? Since when have I let myself be bound by conventions?"

"Then, what?"

"Well, he . . . he kissed me."

He turned and stared at her again. She'd said that so tentatively. "Surely he had kissed you before."

"Yes. Kind of." She made a face. "But this time he tried to get passionate. You know what I mean?"

She really was impossible, but she made him want to laugh. Or at least smile.

"Ashley, he was about to become your husband. I'm sure he was planning on more than the platonic relationship you seem to have had in mind."

"I know." She nodded vigorously, making her hair fly out around her head. "And I thought I was prepared for that. I mean, women can just grit their teeth and close their eyes and bear it if they have to. We all know that."

He groaned, leaning back and laughing. "What a delightfully Victorian philosophy of marriage. Poor Wesley."

"Not that I was planning to do that," she insisted. "That was going to be my fallback position, in case things didn't work out in that regard."

"I see. What a gal. You were really ready for everything, weren't you?"

Her voice lowered mysteriously. "Everything except what actually happened."

He smiled in the dark, wanting to take her in his arms and...and what? He stiffened, turning his thoughts around. There would be none of that. Resolutely, he put his mind back into the conversation.

"And what was that?" he asked.

She hesitated, then moved a little closer on the bench. "Do you remember when you kissed me this morning?" she asked him softly.

Did he remember? He hadn't been able to get it out of his mind all day. "You mean, when you enticed me into kissing you?" he taunted lightly.

Her eyes opened wide with outrage. "You're going to blame me for that?"

"Why not?"

"You were at least as much to blame as I was."

Oh, brother. If he let her, she would go on all night about that damned kiss.

"Okay," he said impatiently. "I'll accept responsibility. I kissed you. Go on."

This was going to be the hard part. She took a deep breath and forced herself to go on. "Well, when you kissed me, I—I felt something." She stopped, too embarrassed to go on.

He moved awkwardly. "Ashley, you're thirty years old. Do I have to explain the physical nature of heterosexual attraction to you?"

"But that's just it. When Wesley kissed me—I was standing there in my wedding dress, and he was looking very handsome in his tuxedo, and he said something actually pleasant and took me in his arms and kissed me—and it was as though I had stuffed my face into a pillow. There was nothing there. Nothing at all."

"I thought you were prepared for that."

"I thought so, too. But when I came face-to-face with it, so to speak, I panicked. I knew I couldn't marry Wesley, and I thought maybe there was something wrong with me. But this morning, when you kissed me..."

"Yes?" he prodded when she stopped.

"I think you should kiss me again," she said quietly.

That wasn't something he would be reluctant to do. Not in a good cause, anyway. As long as that was what they had here.

"Why?" he asked.

"Just so I can see...."

See what? If it turned her on? He laughed shortly. He already knew the answer for himself. "You want me to kiss you as an experiment in your libidinous responses?" he asked, his voice laced with scorn.

"I think so," she said doubtfully. "If that means what I think it means."

"Ashley..."

"Just once." She tapped her forefinger to her lips. "Right here. Just so I can see."

She still hadn't said exactly what she wanted to "see," but he was pretty sure he knew. This was ridiculous. He should get up and walk into the house and stop this nonsense right now. But somehow his legs wouldn't move, and somehow he found himself turning toward her, his heart beating just a little faster.

His lips touched hers tentatively this time, as though he meant to just caress her softly and quickly, then draw back. But things didn't turn out quite that cut-and-dried. The moment his mouth closed over hers, she felt it again, the surge of power, the quickening of her pulse, the sense of thrill, and she clung to him, insisting on more.

Without ever meaning to, he responded. One hand cupped her chin, holding her to him, and his free hand reached back to plunge into her hair, taking control at the back of her head.

It was a glorious feeling. She was sailing on a dream, flying. His hands made her feel so protected, she felt she could let her consciousness drift, let him take over the vertical and the horizontal. Her tongue reached into the warmth of his mouth, and his responded. Wet heat. She'd never known it could be so hauntingly necessary to her survival.

His movements were slow, achingly slow, and she pressed closer, wanting more. Fire spread down her neck and into her chest. Another moment...just another moment.

Drawing back, he stared at her as she reached out and touched the palm of her hand to his cheek.

"Thank you," she said breathlessly.

He didn't ask if she'd felt anything. He didn't need to. He'd felt her feeling it, felt her instantaneous response, and he knew there was nothing at all wrong with her reaction setup. She was completely normal. And there was certainly nothing that needed to be said.

"We'd better go inside and have some dinner," he said gruffly, moving as far from her as he could without falling off the end of the bench. "It's getting late."

"Okay," she said, trying desperately to hold back the bubble of laughter that threatened to break away from her throat. This man was special. Whether he knew it or not, kissing him would always be a landmark in her life. She'd never really wanted a man before.

She'd had her share of intimate relationships in her day. Well, maybe not exactly her share, but she'd had a couple. Neither had been particularly fulfilling. Not only had she never been in love, she'd never felt particularly loving with her partners. They were just that—partners in an enterprise she went through with but didn't especially enjoy. She'd never felt the rush of desire before.

Looking at him, she smiled. She was glad she'd met Kam, glad she'd broken into his house. He had to be a magic man. That was all there was to it.

They went into the house and worked together fixing an enormous salad that they only nibbled at. He told her stories of crazy cases he'd taken on in the past, she told him about children's books she'd illustrated, and they were very careful not to touch each other.

And all the while, she kept remembering his kiss.

It doesn't prove a thing, she told herself sternly, except that you're normal after all.

But she knew deep inside that it meant a lot more than that.

"You take the bed tonight," Kam said as they finished up the cleaning job in the kitchen and looked forward to sleep.

"No." She shook her head firmly. "It's your bed. I was perfectly comfortable on the couch last night. I can take that again."

He gazed at her, askance. "If you were so comfortable, why didn't you stay there?"

"So that's it." She gave him a mock look of outrage. "You're just afraid I'll come visit you in the night."

That was exactly what he was afraid of, though he would never admit it. They argued over who would sleep where for another twenty minutes before settling down in just the same places they had slept the night before.

Ashley snuggled into her covers with a lot more confidence this time. She knew she was going to sleep through the night, knew she was almost a different person from the woman who had shivered and cried the night before. She was stronger, more sure of what she was doing. There would be no night terrors this time.

Her resolution lasted just about four hours. This time when she woke, there was no storm raging outside. The night was still. A moon had risen, lending a pearly patina to everything its moonbeams touched. She lay very quietly and watched the pattern the shadows made on the wall.

She wasn't going to go back to sleep. Her body was too tense, her mind too alert. And from somewhere deep inside, that awful feeling was building again. It wasn't fear, exactly. It wasn't depression. But it was a sort of anxiety that wouldn't leave her alone. She needed comfort so badly, it was almost a physical pain.

"I will not go in and bother him again," she said out loud, staring at the ceiling. "I won't. I swear I won't."

The ache grew in her chest. She thought about his kiss, about the way he had stroked the cat, about the way his dark hair fell over his green eyes, and she writhed with a longing she couldn't identify.

I won't, she told herself again, making it into a chant. I won't, I won't.

She clamped her eyes shut and tried to force sleep. She counted sheep. She tried making every part of her body limp, starting with her toes and working up. She got off the couch and did jumping jacks until she was breathing like a buffalo, then crawled back under the covers and stared at the night.

"I won't," she cried, but it was more a mournful wail now, devoid of any sort of backbone. "I can't. Please, don't let me."

Pathetic. That was what she was, and she knew it. But maybe she could do this without him ever knowing about it. After all, she'd slept with him the night before and he hadn't known until he'd woken. What if she slipped in so quietly he didn't know a thing, and then she slipped back out again at the crack of dawn, and he was never the wiser? What if the moon really was made of green cheese that melted in July?

Still, if she was ever going to get to sleep tonight, she was going to have to try it.

Leaving the couch, she walked quietly down the hall, her heart beating. Kam's door was open. She slipped in like a shadow and looked at him. He was sound asleep, his arm flung out, his hair mussed, and he was sleeping on his side, facing out and leaving half the bed empty at his back.

The conditions were perfect. She could do it if she was very careful. Holding her breath, she slid in under the covers and waited, wishing she could quiet the beating of her heart.

Nothing happened. He went on sleeping, and little by little, her heart calmed down. She smiled in the dark. It was going to be okay.

She began to relax, and her eyelids drooped. Sleep was gaining ground. She dipped down into it a few times, growing groggy, and then, just before taking the final plunge that would put her under, she involuntarily stretched out her legs.

Suddenly she was awake again, grabbing her leg, crying out in soundless agony. Not now, she was thinking at the same time. She began massaging her calf muscle as hard as she could with one hand while at the same time stretching out her foot with the other in hopes of stopping the cramp. This was by far the most excruciating pain she'd ever felt, making that dull aching she'd been feeling in her soul fade away into wretched insignificance.

And all the time, she didn't make a sound. Rolling in tortured misery, contorted with pain, she moved a lot. But very quietly.

Still, it was hopeless. She woke him. He reached out, groping in the dark. "What . . . ?" And then he was up, turning, blinking at her in the moonlight. "What the hell?"

"My leg," she cried, pounding on the tight muscle.

He took in the situation at a glance. "Here," he said, grabbing her leg and pulling it out while working at the muscle at the same time. "Relax."

"Relax?" She groaned, writhing in real agony now. "I'm trying, believe me!"

The pain was receding, but only by increments. He worked the muscle hard, kneading with his strong fingers, and little by little, the awful feeling went away.

"You need more potassium," he announced clinically. "Eat bananas."

"Okay," she said weakly. "Anything you say, Doc."

She pulled back her leg and tried it experimentally. "I guess it's okay now," she said. It felt more bruised than anything else at this point. "Thank you."

"You're welcome." He gazed at her cynically. "I suppose you'll go on back to the couch now?"

She hesitated, then turned her urchin look his way. "Do I have to?"

He hesitated. There wasn't anything he would like better than to have her in his bed for the night. But that was just tempting fate, and he was too wise to do that. And so, he steeled himself instead. "You'd better."

Her smile was appealing, and she didn't make a move to leave. "I'll be good," she promised wistfully.

Reaching out, he touched her hair with his long fingers, running down to the ends of the strands, playing with its silky fullness. "But I can't guarantee that I will," he said gruffly, his eyes dark shadows in his hard face.

She shook her head. "I don't need guarantees," she said softly. "Life is a gamble." She took his hand in hers, lacing fingers. "Let me stay, Kam. I can't sleep alone."

He was melting. Here he was, the Iron Man, and he was melting. What was the matter with him? Where had his strength disappeared to? He just had to try a little harder.

"Ashley, I can't give you what you need," he said, his voice strained. "I'm no good at hugging and comforting. I don't do that sort of thing very well."

"I don't need hugs and comfort. I just need to be with someone. Honest, I won't bother you."

"Stay on your side of the bed, then," he said, surrendering and hating himself for it. He pulled his hand away from hers and turned back to his original sleeping position.

"Thanks." She lay back down and sighed happily. "I know I'll sleep well here. Don't even give me another thought."

He grunted. "Right," he said sarcastically.

"Really. I'll be quiet as a mouse. I don't need cuddling, I just need to feel you nearby. That's all."

There was no response, and since he was now lying with his back to her, she couldn't tell if he was even listening to her any longer.

No matter what she said, she wanted more from him. Was he always this way with women? If so, she mused, he must have a pretty lonely love life. She thought for a moment about what he'd said, and then remembered the name of his lost love.

"Didn't you ever comfort Ellen?" The moment the words were out of her mouth she wished she could swallow her tongue. Why had she said such a stupid thing?

She could feel him stiffen beside her, but he didn't say a word. She felt herself turn crimson with shame and tears stung her eyes. She was such a fool.

"I'm sorry," she whispered. "I shouldn't have said that."

"Go to sleep," he whispered back.

But he didn't sound angry, and that cheered her. She lay very quietly and enjoyed his nearness. Time ran slowly by, and her eyelids began to droop.

She was drifting again, almost asleep, when she felt him turn and then toss back again. Her eyes popped open and she looked over at him.

"You're not sleeping," she told him accusingly.

He turned to stare at her in the dark. "I'm well aware of that."

She went up on one elbow. "What's the matter?"

"Oh, I don't know. Something seems to be bothering me."

"What is it?"

He laughed shortly. "You."

"Me?" She giggled. "Cut it out. You're just tense, that's all. Here, I'll rub your back."

He opened his mouth to tell her not to, but before he could get the words out, her small, cool hands were on his back and he was sighing with instant gratification. She had great moves. Her hands felt wonderful.

He closed his eyes and let her go on and on. Those tiny hands seemed to pry each muscle apart individually and give each a proper tuning. He was floating on air. He never wanted her to stop.

He could tell when she was getting tired, and he rolled, suddenly, so that his chest was where his back had been.

"Thanks," he murmured, reaching out to pull her toward him for a kiss.

She bent to kiss him, but she didn't stop there, and then she was coming down on top of him, wrapping herself in his arms and clinging to his body. White noise filled his head. He wasn't thinking any longer. He pressed her to him, his hands running up beneath the shirt she wore, sliding up her sides, marveling at the butter-smooth skin. She arched up and her shirt fell open. He lifted his head without hesitation, taking the exposed nipple into his mouth. He felt her shudder and his body hardened like molten lava turning to rock.

She heard herself sighing, only it was more than a sigh. It was more like a little animal sound. Her legs wrapped around him and she pressed herself closer, wanting to take him in, wanting to feel the magic she knew he could conjure up in her.

Suddenly he was pulling away. She watched him go, bewildered. "What is it?" she asked groggily, her body aching to have him back. "Where are you going?"

He looked back, shaking his head. How could he have acted like such a Neanderthal? He'd been ready to take what he could get from her, hadn't he?

But then, he thought again, looking down at where she lay, that wasn't right. It hadn't really been like that. He'd been ready to make love with her. That was more like it. Even so, he would have to watch it. That was something he wasn't going to allow himself.

"I am going to take a cold shower," he told her as he turned toward the bathroom. "A very, very cold shower. In fact, if I can find a setting for ice cubes, I may use that."

The cold water did more than tame his libido. It helped bring up memories he needed to take a look at.

Ellen. It had been five years since she'd died. Five very short years, full of hard work and too many cases, too many trials, too much stress. He wished there was a way to pull back, to take on a lighter load, to accept easier cases.

"Take Fridays off," Jill, his secretary was always saying. "Only work mornings. Take up golf. Do something to round out your life before you kill yourself."

But he couldn't. He had always thrown himself into whatever interested him at the moment. He had to do things all the way. He had to immerse himself in them completely. That was just the way he was. And for the past fifteen years or so, his obsession had been the law.

He loved the law. He didn't always love what the law did, or how it sometimes seemed to get twisted in the hands of unscrupulous attorneys, but he loved the theory of it, the philosophy behind it. The law was just about perfect—cool, clear, unemotional and logical—until people came along to muck it up.

Ellen had been just the opposite of that. Wild, chaotic, impulsive, careless. What had attracted him to her? He didn't know. They said that opposites attracted, but he'd never believed that. Until Ellen.

That day when she'd gone out in the sailboat alone, they'd had their worst fight ever. They'd planned to go for a sail together. And then he'd come upon a complication in a case, and he'd told her he had to work on it. Furious, she'd said ugly things and stormed out to take the sail by herself. She'd never come back. She'd never forgiven him. And he would never forgive himself.

He had vowed never to let that happen again. He refused to be responsible for anyone else. He couldn't handle the consequences, so why should he bother? If people were going to go off and do crazy things that put them in jeopardy, let them go. He didn't want to have a thing to do with it.

Now there was Ashley. He'd never asked her to come waltzing into his life. She'd just come. She'd forced her way in and now she wouldn't leave. Or maybe it was that he didn't want her to go. He wasn't sure which.

The thing about cold water was, you never ran out of it, not like hot water. So you had to make up your mind on your own when the shower was over.

Was it over? And if it was over, what was he going to do when he went back out?

Kam wanted Ashley. He ached with wanting her. But if they made love, he was afraid she would be in him in a way he wasn't sure he could stand. Could he risk it?

He switched off the water and let himself drip dry for a moment before reaching for a towel. Slipping back into his pajama bottoms, he went out into the bedroom.

She was still in his bed, but now she was sprawled across it, her head at one corner, her feet pointing to the other, and she was sound asleep, hugging the mattress as though she could sense his presence there still.

He stood very quietly watching for a few minutes. She was so small, so vulnerable, and at the same time, so ready to take on the world. He had to admit it. He sort of liked her.

Turning away, he headed for the couch. It was time to get some shut-eye himself.

· Seven

Morning was actually Ashley's favorite time in Hawaii. The air was soft and fragrant and full of birdcalls, yet there was also a trembling expectancy, as though something good was going to happen.

Waking up, she threw out her arm and encountered nothing but empty space. Rolling over, she found herself all alone in Kam's bed, and she laughed softly.

"Chicken," she murmured to the empty room. "So you couldn't take it, huh?"

Lying very quietly, she thought about what had happened during the night—and what hadn't. Kam was a strange man, but a man she was learning to respect more and more. She liked him. Liked him better than any man she'd ever known before.

Be careful, her cautious side warned her. *You thought you liked Wesley, too, didn't you?*

That was true. But she'd never liked Wesley in the same way she liked Kam. And she'd never thrilled at the sight of him, or his touch, the way she did with Kam. There was a big, big difference.

Luckily, she wasn't going to have to worry about whether she should marry Kam or not, because he wasn't too likely to bring up the subject. She laughed softly, thinking about it. No, Kam was not a marrying guy. She didn't have to bother her head over that dilemma with him. What a relief.

Sliding out of bed, she went to the drawer where she kept the clothing she'd inherited from Shawnee and pulled out a blue bikini. She dropped the shirt she'd slept in to the floor and pulled on the swimsuit, then stretched and walked out into the living room.

She found Kam sound asleep on the couch. Bending, she dropped a kiss on his unprotected mouth.

"Good morning, lazy," she whispered, laughing down at him. Not waiting for a response, she ran out the front door and down the steps to the sand, then to the shore and the sparkling blue water.

The water made a white plume around her as she charged into the lagoon. She dove out and swam hard, enjoying the coolness of the water, the effort of the swim. She was halfway to the reef when she stopped and floated, looking up at the deep blue sky. Then she turned her face down into the water. Tiny turquoise and yellow fishes flitted by. She could only see them vaguely without goggles, but she caught their color as they turned and flashed away. They reminded her of an old song about tiny purple fishes that ran laughing through a woman's fingers, and she smiled, happy to be here, happy to be part of it all.

But then she remembered why she was here, and her smile faded. Where would she have been right now if she'd married Wesley? They'd been planning a two week stay in Bora Bora. She would have been alone with a man she'd quickly learned to detest. She would have been completely miserable by now, frantically trying to find a way out of her situation, coming up against a stone wall every time. Because once those vows were made, there was no escape clause.

She closed her eyes and gave a small prayer of thanks that she'd had the wherewithal to get out when she had the chance. There were still too many loose ends flapping about for comfort. She was going to have to face her family at some point. She was going to have to go back and apologize to Wesley. But for now, she was just grateful she'd done what she'd done.

But that still didn't leave her with a plan. What was she going to do now? Slink out to the airport and climb on a plane for home?

She took a stroke, feeling the water glide over her body, and she realized she didn't want to go home. Going home meant returning to the life she'd tried to leave by marrying Wesley. Not that it was such a bad life. But it hadn't been a particularly fulfilling life for quite some time. Her illustrating career was doing well, but she could attend to that anywhere. She didn't need to be in San Diego. And, once she stopped to think about it, she realized that she really liked it here. Maybe she would have to find a way to stay.

Sighing, she turned and started to swim back toward shore. Her stomach was rumbling. It was definitely time for breakfast.

She was only about a hundred yards from shore when she saw him coming down the beach. She recognized him immediately, and a chill ran through her.

"Eric," she breathed. "Oh, no!"

She had a choice. She could either swim out to the reef and take her chances with the sharp coral, or she could haul herself up to the sand and make a run for the house, hoping her mother's latest beau wouldn't recognize her from a distance. She actually hesitated for a moment, considering the reef idea. But better sense prevailed and she struggled up to the sand and made a mad dash for the house.

Kam had come fully awake when she'd kissed him, but he didn't follow her out for a swim. He lay for a long time, still feeling the touch of her cool lips to his. He was going to have to get her out of here. This was no good. Already his head seemed to be clogged with her scent, the vision of her lovely form, the sound of her happy voice. If she stayed... Well, a man only had so much strength, and his was feeling very frayed around the edges.

The telephone rang, a shrill, insistent sound that belonged to his life in Honolulu. He didn't move. Let it ring. He knew the answering machine would pick it up.

"Kam, are you there?" came the voice of his partner. "Call me right away. I need some help on the Duncan case."

Kam hit the Off button with so much force, he knocked the machine out of commission.

"To hell with the Duncan case," he said aloud. "To hell with the law."

Sacrilege. He loved the law. But right now, he didn't want to think about it. All he wanted to think about was Ashley.

And that was exactly why it was time to go back. He couldn't stay here any longer. One more day, just a few more hours, and he might be so far in he would never get himself free again. He had to leave now while he still had a chance of making it, of getting away with his emotions intact.

He dressed slowly, putting on khaki slacks and a dark polo shirt. Somehow it felt like a day of reckoning. Yesterday had been fun and impulsive. Today was the day they had to decide about the future.

He turned when he heard Ashley coming back. She burst into the house like a small tornado, almost bowling him over. He looked at her as though she were the bearer of news he knew he didn't want to hear. But she told him, anyway.

"It's Eric," she cried. "I've got to hide. Don't tell him I'm here. Tell him I left out the back way. Tell him I'm your sister. Tell him he's seeing things. Just don't tell him I'm here!" And she spun across the room, heading for the back of the house.

Kam sighed, glad he'd already dressed. He might as well go on outside and meet this head-on.

"Eric," he repeated slowly as he walked. "Who the hell is Eric?"

He sauntered out the front door and down the steps, and found a young man loping his way. Tall and slim, and Viking blond, he had the look of someone who spent a lot of time in front of mirrors. He flagged down Kam before he had a chance to say a thing.

"Hey," he called, short of breath. "Did you see a girl in a bikini run by here?"

Kam looked to the right and he looked to the left, then he shook his head. "What kind of girl?" he asked as though completely at sea with the concept.

"Small and cute, kind of blond flyaway hair," Eric said, coming to a stop in front of Kam and looking at him with interest. "She was wearing a blue bikini."

"Sounds like something I would have noticed," Kam said dryly.

"Oh, you would have noticed her all right." He put a hand over his heart. He was still breathing hard. "Mind if I sit down on your step here to recuperate? I've been running down the beach since I caught sight of Ashley. Darn that girl. She's a real pain to pin down.''

He dropped down to sit on the step, then offered a hand to Kam. "I'm Eric Camden," he said. "I'm staying at the King's Way."

Kam shook his hand gravely. "Kam Caine," he said in return. Then he lowered himself to sit beside the younger man. "How could you tell who it was from that far away?" he asked curiously.

Eric shrugged. "I'd know her anywhere. We've been searching for her for the last two days. You wouldn't believe what happened. She was supposed to get married the other day, but she escaped."

Kam's gaze sharpened. "Escaped?"

"Yeah. The poor groom. You've never seen a man so angry." He slapped his knee, thinking of it. "She confided in me, you know. Told me she didn't want to marry him. And I told her not to do it, if it just didn't feel right. I told her I'd go to Geraldine, Ashley's mother, and take care of everything. I told her what to do, and then she went and did it, and now I can't find her anywhere. You sure you haven't seen her?"

"I'll keep a sharp lookout," Kam responded, wondering when the fellow would tumble to the fact that he hadn't answered one question directly.

But Eric had other things on his mind. He turned to look Kam in the face, his pale blue eyes vacuous. "Hey, you got a cigarette on you? I could sure use a smoke."

"Sorry." He lifted an eyebrow. "Cigarettes and exercise don't really mix all that well, you know."

"Oh, I don't really smoke. I hardly even inhale. But I like to have one now and then to settle me down, you know? But I'm serious about my exercise. Oh, brother, if I even miss a day, I start to feel the bloat starting, you know? That's why I work out. Ever work out with weights yourself?''

Kam could sense a long discussion of deltoids and pectorals coming up and he wanted to do anything he could to avoid that. Instead of answering, he changed the subject back to Ashley.

"So...what is your part in all this? Are you planning to take the groom's place? Do you kind of go for this girl who ran away from the wedding?''

"Who, Ashley?" He laughed. "Not at all. She's a great little gal, but kind of flaky. You know what I mean? Besides, I'm dating her mother."

Kam was speechless and Eric grinned, noting his surprise and seemingly feeling quite proud that he'd stunned him.

"Yeah, you know how it is. A lot of us younger guys are going for older women these days. I mean, why not?" His face was open and guileless. "They know everything about everything. They've been around the block and they know what they're doing. They treat you great. And they have a lot of money. I mean, if I were just working at the local market like my brother, there's no way I ever could have afforded to come to the islands and stay in a place like the King's Way. You know? But Geraldine takes care of everything."

"Interesting," Kam murmured. He was surprised he wasn't more repelled by the things this young man was saying, but he realized it was Eric's personality that kept that from happening. He was so darn open and honest about it, you couldn't help but like him, at least a little.

"I look at it this way," Eric went on. "When you go with a girl, you like something about her. Sometimes it's her eyes. Sometimes it's her laugh. Sometimes it's the way she dances, or kisses, or her sexy voice. Maybe it's her brains. Or her bod. There's always something. So why should money not be a factor to like someone for? It's just another item on the list."

"I suppose it's an ingredient in the whole," Kam said noncommittally.

"Don't get me wrong," Eric warned. "Geraldine's a special lady. I like her a lot. Matter of fact, we may get married."

Kam choked, coughing so hard Eric had to pound him on the back.

"Well, I guess I'd better be going," Eric said once Kam had settled back down. "Listen, if you do see her, will you give me a call at the King's Way? I'd appreciate it. Tell her I really need to talk to her, would you?"

Rising, he turned around and gazed at Kam's house with a narrow-eyed look that spoke volumes, then threw Kam a quick smile, and started off jogging back in the direction from which he'd come.

Kam watched him go, shaking his head. It was possible that this young man wasn't quite as vacant as he pretended to be. Turning, he walked slowly back to the house.

"He's gone," he told Ashley when he went back inside. She was huddled on the bed in his bedroom, leaning against the headboard. She was still in the bikini, but she'd wrapped a towel around her like a blanket.

"I can't believe he showed up here on this beach," she said mournfully, her eyes huge and sad.

He looked at her carefully, analyzing her reaction. What had she expected? Did she really think the rest of the world was going to go away and leave her alone after what she'd done? Had he really expected it himself?

"Why not?" he said to her at last. "You say you went jogging along here every morning before you decided to come live in my house. Why wouldn't others use this path, as well?"

She brushed aside his logic. She wasn't feeling very logical right now. She wanted sympathy, reassurance. "Do you think he'll be back?" she asked, looking up at him with hungry eyes.

The lawyer in him was more into facts and reason than comfort and consolation. "Yes, I do," he said bluntly. "He knows you're here."

She sprang up. "What?"

He gave it to her straight. "He knew you were in here the whole time."

She clasped her hands together, her gaze jumping from one side of the room to the other. "Did he say anything?"

"Not really." He shook his head. "But I could tell."

Her hands went to her face, a picture of tragedy. "Oh, no," she moaned. "He'll be back."

"Yes." Kam was sure of it. "He's going to be back, and he's going to bring your mother with him."

One more tremulous wail, and her mourning period was over.

"Okay," she announced, springing into action. "Then I'd better get out of here. Can I take the blue sundress with me? Do you think Shawnee would mind? Where did I put my shoes? At least you don't need to loan me any money, because I've got all that cash I won yesterday."

He took hold of her arm and pulled her back to face him. "No, you don't," he said firmly. "You're not going to run this time. You're going to stay and face this thing."

Her eyes widened tragically. "I can't. Oh, Kam, you don't know how it is. You don't know how they'll suck me back in. I can't stay."

He was nodding at her, still holding her arm. "Yes, you can. I'll be right here with you. They can't make you go with them. You're a thirty-year-old woman. You can do what you want."

But she was shaking her head, hardly hearing him. "You don't know how it is when I get around them. I turn back into a little girl, part of the family, and I can't break free of that. Kam, don't make me do this. I'm not strong enough."

He didn't want to make her do it. He knew what it meant. Whether or not she stood up to them, she would be lost to him. No matter what they did now, the outside world had come in and was about to take over.

For just a moment he had a fantasy of taking her and running. They could go to the mainland, maybe get an apartment in San Francisco. Or they could take a sailboat to Australia. Maybe just go to Honolulu and hide out in Waikiki.

But that fantasy didn't last as long as smoke from a cigarette. It was impossible. He had to get back to his law practice, and she had to face her fears and learn to stand up to them. Besides, he was thinking as though they were lovers, and they weren't quite that. Now they probably never would be, and that was all to the good. Wasn't it?

Looking down into the crystal caverns of her eyes, he wasn't so sure. He could get lost in there. Just one step, one move, and he could change their status forever. A surge of wild temptation flooded him, and he hesitated, wanting to kiss her so badly, the need burned inside him.

He was about to lose her. That much was evident. Yesterday morning, he would have welcomed that. But not now. Still, trying to strengthen the bond between them at this point would only make that more painful. He had to resist, and he knew it. Drawing back, he turned away.

"I'll go rustle us up something for breakfast," he said, his voice rough. "Why don't you change out of that wet suit and join me?"

She didn't say a word. Standing there in the middle of the bedroom, she watched him go, and something broke inside her, broke and let loose a flame that consumed her from deep within.

She knew even better than he did that once Eric returned with her mother in tow, this space in time they'd inhabited would very likely be shattered. There would be no going back, no holding on. She would either have to return to the life she'd interrupted by running away, or she would have to move on to some other place. Staying with Kam was not likely to be an option.

Unless . . . unless . . .

The thought of leaving him behind gnawed at her painfully. She'd never known a man like him and she was pretty sure it would be a cold day before she found another who filled her imagination this way. How could she even contemplate letting him go without a fight? For the first time in her life, she wanted a man. Why wasn't she doing anything about it?

Walking slowly, she went down the hall and stopped in the doorway of the kitchen. Kam turned from the counter and looked at her, and the moment he looked into her eyes, he knew.

"Ashley," he said softly, shaking his head. "No. Don't do this."

But he couldn't move away. He couldn't turn on his heel and head out the back door to get away from her, away from the situation he knew was brewing.

She didn't say a word. Instead, she started toward him.

Head back, eyes half closed, he watched her come.

"Ashley," he murmured, his doubts revealed in his face.

And then she was in front of him, and she reached out and laid the flat of her hand against his chest, and at the same time, her gaze held his. She wasn't asking any longer. She was letting him know what she intended to do. Her eyes were dark and clouded, as though some inner self had taken over.

"Ashley," he repeated, shaking his head.

But she could feel him trembling beneath her hand, and she smiled. "Tell me you don't want me," she whispered, the pounding of her heart vibrating her words. "Tell me you don't want me, and I'll go back to the bedroom and leave you alone."

He couldn't possibly tell her any such thing. He wasn't strong enough for that. Besides, nature was taking over. He was like a tree, and she was the wind. What she began, he would finish. And once he'd made that surrender, he gave himself over to the passion that had been leashed inside him since the first night she had arrived.

He wanted to go slow, to stroke and pet her, to give her a sense of romance that the act should have. But he'd been holding back too much, and now it spilled out, taking him to the edges of control, sweeping her along with it. If he didn't have her, right now, right here, he would split in two in a long, agonizing descent into hell.

His mouth took hers as though he had to fight for it, even though they both knew it was being freely offered. He plunged inside, pouring heat down her throat, sending sensation spinning through her. Her hands took his face between them, and she opened to him in a way that made sure he knew she was his for this moment in time.

His breath was coming faster and faster. He ripped away the top of her bikini and took the still-damp flesh in his hands, caressing her breasts, tugging at the nipples. She arched back, wanting to feel his hot mouth on her cool skin. He touched her with his lips, his tongue, and she moaned, fingers digging into his shoulders, pulling him closer, harder against her. His hands slid down and pushed away the bottom of the swimsuit, and at the same time, her hands began to work at the belt of his slacks.

"Where?" he asked harshly, impatience tearing at his composure.

"Here," she said, leading him the few steps to the table. There was no time to go anywhere else. Their need was too raw, too urgent. Noise filled their heads, sounds like rushing water, rushing blood. All they were was need, all they felt was desire, all they saw before them was the joining that would make them both whole.

She'd never been with a man who wanted her so badly, so intensely, and his need conjured up the same in her. She needed to feel his possession as she needed air to breathe, only more. She had to have him now, or she would surely die.

"Now," she demanded, pulling at him, drawing him closer. "Oh, quickly, Kam. Now, please."

She bent back on the table and he came inside her with a muffled cry that echoed against the kitchen walls. She didn't have time to analyze it. She was filled with a driving, pounding desire that took over her mind and her soul. She cried out, too, urging him on, and her fingers dug into his back as her legs closed around him. She arched higher, demanding he come deeper, and he did as she urged, holding her hips with his hands, holding on to her as though he were afraid she would slip away if he didn't.

She couldn't breathe. She didn't want to breathe. All she wanted was Kam, again and again, taking her higher with each move he made, dragging her with him into the spiraling ecstasy she'd never known before. Something exploded and the tiny lights from cascading fireworks seemed to be dropping all around her. She shuddered and held on, and he joined her intensity with his own, holding her tightly against any storm, protecting and cherishing and urging her higher.

And then, finally, they finished the ride together, their arms holding tightly, their bodies melded together by the heat.

They didn't spend a lot of time regaining strength. The table was not the most comfortable of places. Kam backed away quickly, letting her up.

"The bedroom," she said, pointing the way. "It's not ten steps away. Did we forget?"

He smiled and swung her up into his arms. "The bedroom," he agreed. "The kitchen is for cooking. We're going to have to learn to keep that straight."

"And the bedroom is for making love," she whispered as he laid her down on the bed and came down beside her.

He looked at her creamy skin, the dark nipples, the slim legs, and he felt the quickest renewal he could remember. She saw it, too, and laughed in a rich, deep voice she hadn't had before.

"Again?" she asked, reaching out to touch him.

"Again," he murmured, burying his face in her thick hair. And as his hands stroked her gently this time, teasing her breasts, massaging her stomach, sliding between her legs, her hips began to move, and she sighed her acceptance. But he was going to take it slowly this time. She deserved that, he thought. He would touch her, pet her, arouse her softly, take his time.

But he hadn't counted on Ashley's impatience. She didn't have to be wooed. She was ready almost as soon as the touching began, and she told him so in no uncertain terms. Moments later he was inside her again, and she was crying out with each stroke, arching into his thrusts and savoring the joy as much this time as she had before.

They lay panting, bodies still tangled. Little by little, they regained their breath and composure. Ashley closed her eyes and wondered why she'd never been let in on this wonderful secret before. Making love could actually be enjoyable. Why hadn't anyone ever told her?

It had taken Kam to unlock that particular door. When she looked at him, she was overcome by a sense of tenderness that filled her with a peace and a delight such as she'd never known before. A thought came to her, stunned her with its surprise. Was this love? Could she possibly be in love?

If not, it had to be the closest she was ever going to get to it. And she liked it. She liked it very much.

"I hope they never come back," she murmured, lying in his arms. "I hope a hurricane comes and they get hit by a slight bolt of lightning and lose all memory and forget that I exist." She raised herself up on one elbow and looked at his handsome face, loving the lines, the tan color, the green eyes and the wonderful, luxuriously dark lashes.

"Would you let me stay here?" she asked teasingly. "If they forgot all about me, would you let me stay and swim every day and do my work out under the arbor in the backyard?'' She smiled at him, brushing his hair back. "And you could go to Honolulu every Monday to work and then come back here on weekends, and we could spend all day in bed.'' She dropped a kiss on his temple. "It would be heaven. Until you grew tired of me, of course.''

He pulled her down against him again. "Who said I would grow tired of you?'' he asked gruffly. "Something tells me you would never get to be a bore, Ashley. No matter how hard you tried.''

She sighed happily. She'd never felt so at peace. This was the way life ought to be. Everyone should have a man like this at home. Too bad you had to marry them to make sure they stayed. Too bad she was so bad at relationships.

Some of her joy fled as she let reality come flooding back. Just two days ago, she'd been about to marry one man, now she was making love with another. What kind of floozy was she, anyway?

The truth hurt. She wasn't exactly a good role model. But this thing that she had with Kam was a once-in-a-lifetime situation, and she was glad she grabbed for the happiness it could bring while she could. That didn't make her a terribly wonderful person. But it did make her human.

Eight

They showered and dressed and went to the kitchen to sit stiffly at the breakfast nook and await the visitors they were sure were coming. They were both quiet now, filled with apprehension. Eric and Geraldine were bound to come soon. And then what?

The front door sounded, but it was only Shawnee, back again, this time with lunch.

"I've got sushi," she announced, throwing the bag with the vinegared rice in black seaweed rolls down on the table. She looked at Ashley with a smile, then turned to aim a major wink at her brother.

"Do you always bring food?" Ashley asked her, laughing.

"Always," Shawnee assured her. "That way I know I'll always be welcome." She grinned. "It's a conditioning experiment, like Pavlovian dogs."

"Yeah," Kam said dryly. "People hear Shawnee's coming and they start to drool."

"Kam!"

"Never mind," Shawnee told Ashley. "I'm used to his teasing." She smiled, looking her up and down. "I brought you some more clothes," she said. "Those old castoffs of mine don't really fit too well. So I stopped by Marguerite's Closet and bought you a few things."

"Oh, thank you." But she turned puzzled eyes to her friend's sister. "But how did you know I was still here?"

"Word gets around." Shawnee grinned. "I must have heard the story of how you dominated the pool room at the bar and grill from about five different people. And each of them also told me how Kam came in and took you away. You two are the talk of the town."

"Especially when you run gossip central out of your own restaurant," Kam noted. "If there's no good rumor of the day, she'll start her own."

"Untrue," Shawnee said serenely. "But I know how you like to kid, little brother." She slid in beside Ashley and smiled. "Now, let's break open the sushi."

"You go ahead and eat," Kam said, sliding out and looking restless. "I think I'll go out and take a walk on the beach."

They watched him disappear and Shawnee raised a questioning eyebrow to Ashley.

"We're both a little nervous," she explained. "We're waiting for my family to show up and try to make me go with them."

"Ah." She sat back and looked at her companion, not sure what that meant but interested in other aspects at the moment. "So, despite all disclaimers, you two are officially an item, are you not?"

Ashley smiled demurely, poking at the sushi with curiosity. "You might say that."

Shawnee crowed with delight. "I *will* say that! I'll tell it to the trees." She threw an arm around Ashley and hugged her close. "Thank you, dear beautiful person, for coming to my rescue. I thought I was never going to find a woman for my infuriating brother."

"Oh, we're not getting married or anything like that," Ashley said quickly, looking concerned. It was best to get these things out in the open right away so you didn't disappoint people. After what had happened with Wesley, she was going to be very careful about these things.

"No, no. Of course not." Shawnee shook her head vigorously. "I wouldn't dream of thinking such a thing." Smiling like a Cheshire cat, she went right on and did it, anyway.

"Good." Ashley reached for her set of chopsticks. "Because neither one of us is the marrying kind."

"Right." Shawnee kept her look of skepticism to herself as she fished out her favorite variety of sushi. She took a bite and looked at Ashley speculatively.

"Do you want to hear about what sort of baby he was?" she asked at last. "And his first day at school?" She gave Ashley a superior look. "I've got pictures with me."

The chopsticks dropped from Ashley's hand. "Where?" she said eagerly. "Was he horribly cute? Do you have something of him in diapers?"

Shawnee grinned and reached into her huge purse to pull out the photo album. "I've got everything you want right here," she told her. "Just hold your horses."

They had a lovely lunch, poring over the scraps and images of Kam's childhood. By the time they'd finished looking through the album, Ashley felt as though she'd known him forever.

"He was such a serious child," she noted, sighing as she put away the last picture.

"He's a serious man," Shawnee noted. "But that's partly because of what happened with Ellen. Do you know about Ellen?"

She nodded. "I know a little. I know she died."

Shawnee looked at her for a moment, then decided to say it. "Yes, she did die, in a sailing accident. And he thinks it's his fault. He hasn't had a real relationship with a woman since." Then her smile was back. "Until now."

Bouncing up, she reached for the album. "I've got to get going. I've got some sushi for Cousin Reggie. He's sitting out on a cliff, waiting for his mermaid."

Ashley frowned. "What?" she asked.

Shawnee waved the subject away. "Never mind. I'll explain later. Just remember this, Ashley. My offer for a job still holds. Any time you need a place to stay, give me a call. Okay?"

Ashley slid out to walk her to the door. "I'll remember that. And, Shawnee—" she threw her arms around the woman and hugged tightly "—thank you so much for everything. Especially for being my friend."

Shawnee hugged back and when she pulled away she was a little choked up. "Anytime, Ashley," she said, patting her. "Anytime." And as she turned to go, she began whistling a happy tune.

Kam came in shortly after his sister left, but he wasn't whistling. In fact, he didn't even look very happy. He found Ashley cleaning up the dishes and he leaned against the counter to vent his problems.

"We have to have a serious talk," he told her solemnly.

She glanced up, but went on cleaning. "About what?"

"About the fact that we made love without protection."

She turned to stare at him, then tried to smile. "I felt very protected."

"You know what I mean. We didn't use anything."

She wasn't sure she liked this conversation. They'd had a wild and wonderful encounter. She knew it was only sensible and smart to use birth control, especially a barrier kind. But she didn't want to think about things like that now. She wanted to hold the warmth of that wonderful morning to her heart and keep it safe forever.

"I thought swinging bachelors like you always had that sort of thing handy," she said lightly, hiding how she felt.

"My swinging days were long ago," he told her.

She looked up into his eyes. "Before Ellen?" she guessed.

This time she didn't even startle him. "Yes," he said evenly. "Before Ellen."

She took his hands in hers and looked into his eyes. "Kam, did you love her very much?" she asked, scared of the answer but needing to hear it.

Looking at Ashley's face, he wondered. Did he love Ellen? He'd thought he had at the time. But now he was finding a whole new realm of feeling with Ashley that he hadn't known was out there waiting for him. And that made him wonder. He hedged. "We thought we were in love."

"Shawnee says you felt more responsibility than anything else."

He nodded, his mouth twisting with annoyance that his sister had been discussing his life. "She might be right about that," he said shortly. "Whatever else, I know it was my fault."

She searched his gaze, trying to find evidence of mercy, a mercy he might show to himself. "But she died in a sailing accident. How could that be your fault?"

His eyes were tortured, there was no getting around it. "I let her go."

"But—"

"I was angry with her. She was angry with me. I'd promised to take her sailing, and when it came time to go, I wanted to finish up some briefs. She had a very short fuse, and that got her going right away. We had a screaming fight, and she went off to go sailing by herself. I knew it wasn't safe. I should have stopped her."

She stood before him, holding his hands, and she didn't know what to say. "Would you be married to her today if the accident hadn't happened?" she asked at last.

He thought for a moment. "I don't know. I doubt it." Then he looked at her and shook his head. "You're sure a nosy one. Why do you have to know all this?"

She shrugged. "I want to know everything about you," she said simply. "From baby pictures to what you want for dinner."

He warmed to her, dropping a kiss on her lips. "You got me off the subject," he complained.

"What subject?"

"The risk we took today. We have to talk about the fact that we didn't use protection."

"Oh, yeah." She shrugged it off. "Don't worry about it."

He looked disturbed by her attitude. "But I will worry about it. If anything happens, I want you to call me right away. I'll help you. It's my responsibility."

"Oh." She glanced at him and then away. Responsibility. That was all he seemed to want to talk about. She didn't want to be a burden to him, something he viewed as a duty. She wanted to be fun for him, a day in the park, red balloons and cotton candy. And all he could see was the ticket price and whether or not there was parking.

But something else he said bothered her, too. She frowned, thinking it through, then turned to ask him.

"You said I should call you. Where are you thinking you're going to be?"

He looked as though he were surprised she didn't see the obvious. "Back in Honolulu. I live and work there, you know."

"Yes. I know." But she wished she could forget it. "When are you going back?"

His grip on her hands tightened. "I'm supposed to go back tomorrow."

A knife cut through her heart, but she survived. Smiling bravely, she asked, "Where will I go?"

She was asking herself, not him, but he answered, anyway. "Why don't you stay here?"

She looked around herself as though she'd never thought of that. "Here?"

"You can stay in this house for as long as you want. Live here. I hardly ever come here more than once a month. There's a housekeeper who keeps things in order and the refrigerator stocked, and there's a gardener who keeps the yard in shape.''

This seemed a lot like the dream she'd expressed earlier, only the heart of that had been his presence every weekend. That seemed to be missing from the scenario he was setting. And, anyway, that had just been a dream. Stay here? She wasn't sure about that.

''I don't think so,'' she said slowly. ''I think I'll have to look for another solution.''

And what was the use in thinking about it? She was probably going to be back with her parents by tomorrow. *C'est la vie.*

He read her mind. ''You're not going back, Ashley,'' he told her firmly. ''You're going to stand up to them.''

Her smile wavered. ''Easier said than done, *mon ami,*'' she murmured. ''We'll see.''

It was only moments later when she heard them coming. Ashley stiffened, her heart pounding so hard it hurt. Dashing to the window, she looked out. There they were, coming up the walk, Eric way ahead of her mother. And, as usual, she felt the same old mixture of love and aversion.

She wanted to run from this, run far and away and never have to face them. But Kam said she should meet this with strength and dignity, and she knew he was right, so here she went. Steeling herself, she walked out onto the porch.

''Hi, everybody,'' she said cheerfully.

Eric was almost up to the house. Her mother was straggling somewhat behind.

''Thank God, it's you, Ashley,'' Eric cried when he spotted her. ''I knew you had to be in here.'' He stopped and stared up at her, hands on his slim hips.

"Will you tell your mother why you ran away? She's driving me crazy with the accusations, day and night. She thinks it's my fault. Tell her I didn't help you do it. Did I help you? No. So tell her already."

Ashley looked toward where her mother was struggling up the walk, breathing hard.

It was the same old thing. Sometimes she felt like a squabbling child, sometimes she felt like an impatient parent herself. But always, no matter how much she railed against her, she loved her mother. You just couldn't get away from that, could you?

"Eric had nothing to do with this, Mother," she called out. "I did it all on my own."

Geraldine came to a stop and mopped her brow before speaking. An older, handsome woman, she was well-preserved and expensively bejeweled.

Kam came out onto the porch in time to hear what she had to say. So this is Ashley's mother, he thought to himself. Going on the theory of like mother, like child, Ashley was in for quite a few more good years.

"I just can't accept that," Geraldine was saying in answer to Ashley's statement. She looked at her daughter from behind jet-dark glasses. "I just can't believe you would do that to your mother."

"I didn't do it to you, Mother," Ashley reminded her, suppressing the flare of panic that was always there at the idea of having disappointed her parent. "I did it to Wesley and to his parents, and I'm very sorry, but if my wedding were today, I'd do it again."

Her mother rolled her eyes. "It's been just terrible, Ashley," she went on as though her daughter hadn't said a word. "How could you do this to us? I just don't understand."

Ashley wanted to cover her ears and curl up into a ball and avoid this criticism. It hurt. It brought up memories of childhood she would rather not relive. Ashley turned and looked at Kam for support. He stepped forward and took her by the elbow.

"Mrs. Carrington, I'm Kam Caine, and this is my house," he said calmly. "Why don't you and your friend come in and sit down?"

Geraldine stared at him. "Yes, why not?" she said faintly, as though she were still trying to figure out just who he was and what he had to do with all this.

They came inside and sat down, Geraldine and Eric on the couch, Ashley and Kam on chairs facing them, and Geraldine went on as though there had been no interruption.

"This has been so awful, Ashley. Why, I don't know what to say to Jean Butler. We've always been such good friends, but when your daughter jilts your friend's son, relationships can be torn apart, you know. There is bound to be a certain amount of resentment released. I just can hardly face her now. She had that lovely luncheon for me yesterday, to introduce me to all her local friends, and here all these people came to stare at me. No one dared ask me what my daughter could possibly be thinking of to do such a thing. But they were all thinking exactly that. And they all just sat and stared at me, every single one of them."

Ashley smiled nervously, pushing her hair back behind her ear. "Why didn't you cancel the luncheon?" she suggested sensibly.

"Cancel the luncheon?" Geraldine batted her soft brown eyes, looking bewildered. "But it had been set weeks ago. Everyone had been invited. How could we cancel it?"

Ashley gave Kam a see-I-told-you-so look and said, "Mother, when there is a natural disaster, or an escape from a wedding, things can be canceled at the last minute.''

Geraldine waved that blasphemy away with a flick of her wrist. ''I never heard of such a thing,'' she insisted. ''We couldn't cancel. And it was a lovely luncheon, except for the staring.''

A hysterical giggle was trying to make its way up Ashley's throat and she had to struggle hard to keep it down. Eric suddenly went into a coughing fit and Kam had to show him to the kitchen where he could get a drink to clear it up. Meanwhile, Geraldine leaned forward to tell Ashley something in confidence.

''Eric is not working out well,'' she confided in a loud whisper. ''Not well at all.''

That giggle was getting more insistent. ''Oh, really?'' Ashley responded faintly, glad Kam had left the room. If she'd met his eye on this one, she wouldn't have been able to hold back the laughter. ''What a shock.''

''No, I thought he would be perfect, but it seems that is just too much to ask.'' She sat back and fanned herself with a magazine, still overheated from her effort to keep up with the younger man on the trip over. ''It's a shame, you know. And he seemed so loving at first.''

Ashley sighed, managing to settle down, and looked at her mother sympathetically. ''Maybe if you picked an older man—'' she began.

''Ashley, darling,'' her mother cut in, as though speaking to a half-wit. ''Haven't you noticed? Most older men want younger women. Don't you think if I could find an older man, a man of breeding and dignity, someone I could actually talk to once in a while, someone who would actually understand what I was saying, that I wouldn't snap him up in a heartbeat?''

She snapped her fingers to illustrate her point. "Of course, I would. But no. They all want young, nubile Barbie dolls. Just look at your father." Her blue eyes flared with the outrage of it all. "So, what the heck, I always say. Older men get younger women with money. I've got money. Why shouldn't I do the same?"

Ashley reached out and took her hand in both of hers. "Because you're not enjoying it very much," she noted softly.

Geraldine threw back her head. "Oh, I wouldn't say that. There's a special little thrill now and then, when you can make people's heads turn. That's sort of fun." She squeezed Ashley's hand with her own, as though to acknowledge the sympathy and thank her for it. "And one does need an escort to certain functions. Eric is handy for that."

Suddenly her mask of superiority fell away and her eyes were clear and filled with the vulnerability she lived with every day. "That's why I want to see you happily married, darling, so you don't have to go through these things."

A lump was suddenly hindering things in Ashley's throat, but she cleared it away and looked at her mother lovingly. "Mother, you're a beautiful woman. And more than that, you're a bright, intelligent woman with an intellectual curiosity and a warmth that has hardly been tapped. I wish you'd value yourself a little more. You deserve to." She took a deep breath and came to the point. "You don't need Eric."

To her surprise, her mother didn't get angry. She sighed and nodded her head. "I know that. And you're right. You're right. I have to get myself together and take charge of my life." Smiling tremulously, she pulled her daughter to her on the couch and held her in her arms. "Oh, Ashley, Ashley, I always feel so much better after I talk to you."

Kam was watching from the doorway. He'd seen a lot of the last exchange, and everything about it surprised him. He'd expected to see Ashley revert to being a little girl, cowed by her mother, unable to act like an adult around her. But what he was witnessing was nothing like that. It seemed the family relationships were actually a little more complex than he had assumed.

Eric shouldered his way past him in the doorway, his coughing spell taken care of. "Now, have we settled things?" he asked the two women, noting their continuing embrace. "Good, it looks good. Are you coming back with us, Ashley? Shall I get your things?"

"Oh, hush, Eric," Geraldine said, turning to face him. "We've hardly begun to discuss it."

"But I've got a tennis date at two," Eric said, coming over to stand above Geraldine and whining like a little boy. "I don't want to be late. Can't we hurry this up?"

Geraldine took his hand much as she might have with her own son. "We'll take this at its own pace, Eric. You'll just have to be patient."

There was a scuffling sound outside, and moments later an older man burst into the room through the front door that had been left open. Right behind him was a voluptuous young woman in a revealing sunsuit. Her pouty look indicated her position. The man was dressed in white shorts and a white polo shirt. Despite his receding hairline, he was a handsome man whose manner bespoke a certain sort of casual power.

"Aha!" he cried upon spotting Geraldine and Eric. "There you are!"

"Oh, hush, Henry," Geraldine remonstrated. "You sound like something out of a nineteenth-century melodrama."

"Well, you act like you belong in a nineteenth-century melodrama. Poor, pitiful Pearl. Always a tragedy in your past and a harebrained scheme for your future." He threw a look of disgust Eric's way. "What's next, Geraldine? Are you going to be living in a grass shack and going fishing for your dinner off the coral reef?"

Geraldine's eyes flashed fire. "If Eric and I decide to live that way, we will live that way, and it will be none of your business."

Suddenly, Henry caught sight of Ashley. Rushing forward, he took her in his arms and gave her a giant bear hug. "There's my girl, my pumpkin, my littlest angel." Still holding tight, but leaning his head back, he looked at her sadly, shaking his head. "Oh, my baby, what have you done?"

"Daddy." Ashley struggled to get free.

"How could you do this?" her father went on, throwing himself into full lecture mode. "Poor old Wesley. He's a broken man, Ash, a broken man. He's a lost soul in shock. He's wandering around like a man whose days are numbered."

"Is he really?" she asked him doubtfully. Somehow this image of Wesley didn't fit anything she knew about the man.

"Well..." Christina, her father's girlfriend, begged to differ, as she usually did. "Your father isn't quite accurate on that one. Wesley's acting weird, all right, but I wouldn't say he was exactly grieving."

Christina probably couldn't imagine any man grieving over any other woman than herself. "It was pretty exciting there for a while. After he realized you were really gone, he ran around the house and broke all your pictures. Then he threw your clothes out the upper window onto the lawn. That was pretty funny. He fired the groundskeeper because he didn't stop you. And he was going to fire the maid, but it turned out she'd been in the family for twenty years and his mother wouldn't let him." Her giggle turned into a hiccup. "It was a kick. Really."

Ashley frowned thoughtfully. "So, what you're saying is, he was more furious than sad."

"Yeah," Eric chimed in, laughing along with Christina. "He looked more like a good ol' boy with a picked pocket than a lover with a broken heart."

"Eric," her mother admonished. "That is hardly accurate."

"Let him say it," Ashley said with a faint smile. "It's honest. We need more honesty in this family." She looked at each of their faces, one by one. "Don't you think?"

The silence that greeted that suggestion was a story unto itself. Reaching out, her mother took her hand again, and smiled encouragingly.

"Well, it's all over now. You've had your time to think. I'm sure you've come to the right decision and you're ready to go back and do the right thing. Isn't that right, darling?"

Ashley pulled her hand away from her mother and looked at Kam, a desperate flare in her eyes. "We haven't really talked this over yet," she said weakly.

"There will be plenty of time to talk when we get back to the hotel room. We'll have a lovely afternoon tea by the pool. Would you like that? Then we can call the Butlers and make up with them, too."

Ashley looked at her hands and didn't speak. Her face was bright red, but Geraldine didn't seem to notice as she went on.

"We'll take you back to our hotel room first. You need to get cleaned up and put on something a little more presentable." She gave the sundress a look of mock horror. "Then we'll call the Butlers...."

"No." Ashley had said it very softly. Everyone stopped and looked at her, but no one was quite sure if she could really have said it.

"...And we'll tell them you want to apologize," Geraldine tried again.

"No." Ashley said it a bit more strongly this time, and everyone heard it. There was a stunned silence, and then Geraldine shook her forefinger at her daughter.

"Of course you'll go back. How can you think anything else? With Wesley you're set for life. You'll have no worries at all. We'll always know where you are."

Ashley sat looking at her hands, shaking her head.

The others all looked at one another. Finally her father stepped forward. "The rest of you go on out and look at the ocean," he said firmly. "I'll handle this."

Geraldine rose. "How unique," she sniffed. "Are you actually going to attempt to take on some of your parental responsibilities at this late date?" But she took Eric's arm and led him out the front door.

"Well, I'm not leaving," Christina announced to all and sundry. "But I do need a drink of water. Don't talk about anything important until I get back, okay?" She flounced out of the room.

Henry sat beside his daughter and put an arm around her shoulders. "I want to talk to you about

Wesley, but I've got to find a way to get rid of Christina for a moment or two,'' he said.

Kam took the hint and slipped back to the kitchen to see if he could keep Christina occupied for a while.

"Oh, Daddy, I'm sorry," Ashley said, "But don't you think this one is really too young?"

Henry started to argue that she was avoiding the subject of Wesley, then looked into his daughter's clear blue eyes and got sidetracked.

"You have a point," he admitted sadly. "It is odd, you know. She's always talking about modeling or she talks about things that bore the hell out of me. And some of the words she uses—it's a foreign language, I swear."

Ashley smiled and patted his hand. "There's a solution to that," she noted quietly, but he didn't seem to hear her. His mind now occupied with his own problems, he went on.

"Do you know, the other day I told her my family didn't have a television when I was growing up and she very wisely noted that that was probably because electricity hadn't yet been invented. *Invented*. That was the word she used."

He sat back against the pillows as though exhausted by the effort of trying to understand the workings of her young mind. "I mean, what does she think, that televisions were sitting around on shelves and no one knew what to do with them until someone rigged up the first wall socket? I swear!"

Ashley laughed.

"I know, I know, she's a cute little thing, but I have to get rid of her."

Ashley glanced at him, startled. "Can't you just tell her to leave?"

He shook his head. "She seems to cling. You know what I mean?"

Ashley thought for a moment. "I have an idea. Get her a modeling job in L.A. She'd be thrilled. And you can swing it. You've got enough contacts to do that. Once she's in the thick of things there, she'll wander off on her own."

Henry frowned. "Do you really think it would work?"

Ashley sighed. If only all of life's bumps were so easily smoothed. "I can practically guarantee it."

Henry began to see the light. He pulled her close and laughed aloud. "You're a genius. Of course. That's exactly what I'll do."

Standing in the doorway once again, Kam had witnessed enough of their discussion to know this was more evidence of what he'd discovered before. Ashley was no puppet being dominated by her family. The things she did for them she did voluntarily. Maybe they had an emotional hold over her, but that was only because she let them. Things were not always as they seemed.

Christina came in from the kitchen, eyeing him in the doorway. "Hey, I thought you said you were coming back to show me how to eat papaya seeds." She wiped at the little black remnants clinging to her chin. "I don't get it. They tasted awful."

"Oh, sorry," he said with a smile. "Maybe it was a male papaya. You have to watch out for that."

She stared at him suspiciously, but before she had time to take him to task, Eric and Geraldine came back in the front door.

"How are things going?" Geraldine asked.

"What?" Henry looked up guiltily, realizing suddenly that he hadn't said a word to his daughter about going back to Wesley. "Uh, you didn't give us enough time," he complained.

Geraldine waved away his protest. "You got sidetracked, as usual, didn't you? Never mind. We don't have all day." Sitting down on the other side of Ashley, she pulled at her hand, demanding her attention.

"Now, darling, you have to go back to Wesley. That's all there is to it. You know your father has business ties with the Butler family. What do you think this will do to his business? He's not getting any younger, you know. He can't start all over again. This is his life. You can't take that away from him. After all, he's the only father you've got."

Ashley stared at her mother, unused to hearing this sort of support for her ex-husband. Henry stared, too.

"Why, Geraldine," he said softly, "I didn't know you thought that way."

"Of course I do," she said sharply. "I care what becomes of you, you fool. I was in love with you once. We made this beautiful daughter together. You can't just throw all that away because of a silly snit."

"Twenty years of divorce seems a bit more than a silly snit," Henry offered, his eyes bright. "But I get your drift, darling."

Geraldine went on, putting on the pressure with practiced ease. "Your father has always been there for you, and now he needs you. You have to come through for him."

They all stared at Ashley, waiting for her to cave in.

"No," she whispered again.

Everyone gasped.

"What?" her mother demanded.

She raised her chin and looked them in the eye. "No," she said, more loudly this time. "No, no, no. I can't. I won't."

"You can't what?"

"Go back to Wesley. I don't love him. I don't even like him. I can't marry him."

"That's impossible."

"I can't. I'm sorry."

The collective outrage could have started a fire by spontaneous combustion. Kam felt it was time for him to step in, and he did.

"You heard her," he said, his arms folded across his chest. "She's staying right here."

Geraldine looked him up and down, finally acknowledging his existence. "What do you have to do with this?" she demanded haughtily.

"I'll tell you," Kam said, staring her down. "You know, we all have our own self interest in this case. But I'm sitting here as an observer, and I've got to say I haven't noticed anyone giving a damn about Ashley's interest. About what she needs, and what will work in her life. All you all care about is your own selfish needs."

He looked around the room, noting who looked guilty and who looked defensive. "So that's what I'm doing," he told them all. "I'm here to look out for Ashley."

"Would you let her go if she wanted to?" Henry demanded.

Kam looked him in the eye. "Of course. It's completely up to her. This has to be her decision."

They grumbled and sputtered, but in time, they drifted away, and finally Ashley and Kam were left alone, watching the last of them disappear down the path.

"What now?" Kam asked her softly.

She turned and looked at him, her eyes luminous. "What now?" she echoed, asking him. "I don't

know. I just don't know." She stepped toward him,
feeling vulnerable. "Hold me, Kam," she said.
"Please hold me."

Ashley and Kam walked down to the town and ate
at a small Italian restaurant where they had known
Kam all his life. The owner played tunes on his accor-
dion and the waiters sang Italian love songs and arias
from great operas. They drank Chianti from green
bottles and ate over a red-and-white checkered tablecloth, gazing at one another over the tops of candles.
Ashley was sure she had never had such a delicious
meal in her life. Kam laughed more than she'd ever
seen him, telling jokes and listening to her crazy stories. They held hands across the tablecloth.

"You know what I'm feeling?" she asked him as
they strolled home under a tropic moon. "I feel as
though we're living in one of those World War II
movies where the enemy is about to invade or the man
is about to leave on a dangerous mission, and the
couple has one last night together. A night to hold in
their hearts forever."

He pulled her close and stared down into her eyes.
"I've never met anyone like you, Ashley," he said, his
heart in his voice. "You're very special to me."

"Ditto, Kam," she agreed, and then she pulled his
mouth down to hers and showed him exactly how she
felt. A word of praise from him was all she needed to
make her completely happy. Was that being in love?
She wasn't sure yet.

She was wearing a long, white, off-the-shoulders
dress that Shawnee had included in the packet of
clothes she'd purchased. Shawnee the Romantic.
Ashley loved her for it. When she first modeled the
dress for Kam, his eyes had glowed and he'd had to

kiss her. Now, on the way home, he had to stop at the drugstore for provisions.

"Protection," he assured her. "We're not making love again without it."

But they did make love again. And again. In fact, the night was waning against a purple sky before either of them got any sleep. After all, this was supposed to be their last night together.

Nine

———

"**I** have to go see Wesley."

Kam sat staring across the table at her, but he didn't say a thing.

Ashley looked up and gave him a tremulous smile. "You know I have to go and see him."

Kam nodded slowly. He didn't say anything, but he was glad she'd come to that conclusion by herself. The better he got to know her, the more he realized that his first impression of her as a silly, willful childlike woman was a grave mistake.

"I'll go with you," he said. "I'll wait outside. Just in case."

She smiled at him, her heart full. "Thank you," she whispered, tears in her eyes. Reaching out, she took his hand. "I'm so glad it was your house I broke into," she added.

"Me, too," he said.

* * *

It was hard going back to the Butler mansion on the top of the hill. It was one of the hardest things she'd ever done. But she walked into the house with her head held high, stopped to say hello to the older Butlers, then went into the study where Wesley was waiting for her.

He sat at the desk and watched her enter, his pale eyes hostile. She stopped a few feet back from the desk.

"Wesley," she said bravely. "I came to tell you that I'm sorry."

He turned slowly in his chair so that he faced her fully. His eyes were without expression. "Sorry doesn't really seem sufficient, does it?" he said quietly.

"No, of course it's not. I did a horrible thing to you. I'll regret doing it all my life. I don't know how I can make it up to you."

He leaned back and looked at her through narrowed eyes. "Marry me," he said coldly.

She hesitated, surprised, not sure what he meant. "Wesley, that's no more possible now than it was the other day. I can't marry you."

He leaned forward, hands clasped on the desktop. "You see, that's what bothers me. Why is it that you can't stand the thought of marrying me?"

She licked her dry lips. "It's not like that."

"Then what is it like?" he demanded. "Do you have any idea what you did to me? I can't sleep. I sit for hours and rack my brain. Why? Why? What is it about me that is so repugnant?"

"Oh, Wesley." She sank into the chair facing his desk. The guilt for what she'd done was suffocating her. "I don't know what I can say...."

"No, of course not. There is nothing you can say."
He squinted at her. "After all, it's not as though I
wanted this marriage any more than you did. But you
didn't see me running at the last minute, leaving you
standing at the altar with everyone whispering all
around you."

Ashley frowned. Had she heard right? "What?"
she asked, seeking clarification.

"Oh, cut the act, Ash. We've known each other too
long. My parents pressured me into our engagement
just like your parents pressured you. We were never in
love, and we both knew it."

Ashley swallowed hard and suddenly wanted to
laugh. My, wasn't she the feeble-minded innocent? It
had never occurred to her that Wesley didn't love her.
How had she been fooled?

"We both knew we were entering into a relationship that was as much a business proposition as it was
a marriage. I was ready to uphold my side of the bar-
gain. But you... you got cold feet and made a run for
it. And you ruined everything."

"Everything?"

"The deals between my father's company and your
father's mortgage brokerage. Didn't they tell you?"

She shook her head, struck dumb.

"Well, they should have. Then maybe you would
have found some other way to turn me loose."

"Oh, yes," she breathed, nodding vigorously. "I
surely would have."

Wesley shook his head, looking at her as though she
were a sorry spectacle. "I know you thought I was
acting beastly toward you these last two weeks," he
said, softening somewhat. "But I was feeling a good
bit of resentment for being tied to this marriage thing

myself. For me, it was too late to back out. But you obviously had other plans."

"No plans." She shook her head, still stunned. "I just knew it was no good."

Wesley stared at her for a moment, then sighed. "Well, maybe it's all for the best. Your father's firm hasn't been doing so well lately. He's spending too much of his time chasing young women. You ought to put a stop to that, you know."

She nodded. "Sure," she said, her voice hoarse.

"And about Kam Caine..."

Her head shot up and her eyes widened.

"Oh, yes, I know all about the new man in your life. You've taken up with an old rival of mine. I can't say that doesn't add salt to the wounds, because it does." His smile held no humor whatsoever. "Know what the Kam is short for? Kamehameha. We used to get a lot of mileage out of teasing him about that one." He laughed shortly. "Tell him he's still a lousy swimmer, and I can beat him at anything else. Except maybe, making you happy." He shrugged. "Go on, Ashley. Go back to your new boyfriend. Have a good life."

She rose, fighting tears of relief. "What will you do?" she asked him.

"I'm taking over our branch in Dallas. I feel the need to get away."

She nodded, then stuck out her hand. "Good luck," she told him.

He took her hand and looked at it. "You, too," he said. Suddenly his grin was wide and warm. "And thanks for doing what I didn't have the nerve to do. Do you realize we would be married now if you hadn't done that?" He grimaced. "Wow. Close shave, huh?"

* * *

"It's hard to believe," Kam agreed when Ashley had filled him in on this change in Wesley. "I guess we all mature over time."

"I wouldn't count on it," she teased, watching him negotiate the car back into the driveway of his house. "And now, we have the rest of the day before you leave tonight. Do you have any plans?"

"Yes." He turned off the engine and looked at her. "I'm booked up today."

"Oh." She was disappointed. "Well..."

Reaching out, he pulled her into his arms. "I have plans to be with you, Ashley." He kissed her soundly, then drew his head back and smiled. "What would you like to do?"

Swim. That was one thing. They swam together like a pair of dolphins, cavorting and laughing and splashing in the water. Then they took a shower together and had fun with the soaping down part. Which led to other things, of course.

Eat. They had a late lunch at a tiny café that sat on a bluff overlooking the sea. Kam fed her grapes, one by one, and Ashley sang him a French song that made him laugh.

Visit. They stopped by Shawnee's restaurant and said hello, and Kam asked his sister if she was willing to loan out her son Jimmy's old VW bug. "But I'm not sure what I'm going to do yet," Ashley protested.

"At least you'll have wheels until you decide," he told her. "I want to make sure you have your own transportation."

Sleep. That was the best part. They took an afternoon nap curled in each other's arms and whispered secrets for an hour or so.

"Tomorrow at this time, you won't be here," Ashley said sadly, lying back against his chest.

He couldn't speak for a moment. "I'll be working," he said at last, a little more gruffly than perhaps necessary. "Are you going to stay here?"

Turning, she looked at him. "I think so," she said softly. "If that's all right. At least for a while." She smiled and played with his hair, digging her fingers into its thick darkness. "I think I'll work at Shawnee's place, at least until I get a new book assignment from my publisher."

"Good." He rolled over and kissed her cheek. "Shawnee will take good care of you."

She wasn't sure why that seemed to make him so happy. He'd been very clear. He wasn't planning to visit her any time soon. He had work to do and he wasn't going to have any free weekends for some time.

She didn't want to ask him about it. He was a free spirit and she knew it. He didn't want to be tied down with promises. Well, neither did she. Or did she? Her own wants and needs were getting more confusing by the minute.

"I'm glad you went to see Wesley today," he said to her as they puttered around the kitchen, fixing their evening meal of shrimp and salad. "Now you can put all that behind you."

"Easy to say," she noted, chomping on a celery stalk. "It just reaffirmed my family's fatal flaw. None of us can sustain a relationship for the length of time it takes to digest last night's dinner. You saw them yesterday. What was your conclusion after seeing my mother and her young boyfriend and my father and his young girlfriend?"

"I thought they were all nuts," he admitted. "You know what? I think your parents are still in love with each other. They just haven't been able to admit it yet.''

Ashley shook her head firmly. "No way. That one has been dead for too many years to count. They're just both congenitally unable to bond, and they passed that annoying trait onto me.''

Kam turned and took her face between his hands, looking deeply into her eyes. "I don't believe that, Ashley,'' he said solemnly. "Not after what I saw yesterday.''

She blinked, looking up into the eyes she was beginning to think she might be in love with. "What did you see, exactly, that I didn't notice?''

He nodded. "I saw you as you are, instead of the way you think of yourself. When I first met you, I thought you were a spoiled rich girl, following her latest whim, flighty and used to getting anything she wanted from her parents as long as she kowtowed to their every wish.''

She considered, head to the side. "There have been times that description wouldn't have been far from the truth,'' she admitted.

"Uh-uh.'' He shook his head, not giving her even that. "I saw something completely different. I saw the way you're always there for them. You always pick up the pieces, don't you?''

She stopped and thought for a moment. "Sort of,'' she admitted.

"You always have. That's why you haven't been able to fall in love and have a relationship of your own. It's not because you're not capable of commitment. I can see you committed.''

"I can see me committed, too. Ever since I've taken up with you I've been expecting the little men in the white coats any minute.''

"Ashley..." He dropped a kiss on her lips. "I'm not joking. You're the glue that holds your family together. But you don't need to be. They can make it on their own, if they would only try. And in the meantime, you should be thinking about starting a family of your own. All you need to do is learn from their mistakes. You'll do fine."

Starting a family of her own. That would be turning her head and making her swoon if only he were talking about a scenario that included him. But she knew that wasn't even in his mind. And so the picture hurt, instead.

"I'll think it over," she said lightly, concealing her heavy heart. And they went back to fixing a meal.

And then it was time for Kam to pack.

A pall fell over their good humor. As she helped him fill his suitcase, she seemed to have forgotten how to tell a joke.

"You've got forty-five minutes until your flight," she said at one point. "I suppose you'd better get going."

"I suppose," he said, lingering one more time.

He kissed her goodbye and she turned away at the last minute so he wouldn't see the tears welling in her eyes. She listened as his rental car left the driveway and turned into the street, and then she went to the bathroom to wash her face and stare at herself in the mirror.

It was over. This small, short, idyllic period, probably the best part of her life, was already over. What was she going to do now?

The front door opened. Her heart leapt into her throat and she dashed out to find Kam in the living room. Racing together, they clung.

"I can take the first flight in the morning," he said breathlessly.

And that was all the explanation she needed. His mouth caught hers and she trembled with anticipation, her hands sliding beneath his shirt to find the flesh she was beginning to know so well.

Her dress seemed to fall away of its own accord. His large hands caressed her skin, gliding over every curve and finding every secret hiding place.

But she didn't have any secrets from him any longer. Her body was his. He was the only one who had ever mastered it, the only one who had ever found the mysteries and brought them to the surface. She needed him to guide her to fulfillment, because she'd never found it with any other man.

His hunger for her was a demand that sent a thrill cartwheeling through her, a demand she wanted to meet with the urgency of her own. The couch was waiting. They fell onto it, bodies intertwined as though they meant to tie a knot together.

She reached for him, felt his strength, his power, and shuddered with the desperate necessity of possessing him. He took her with a sweeping sense of drama that sent her senses reeling. She was hardly human any longer, she was a spirit, a piece of the wind, a force of nature who must dance to nature's tune or pay the consequences.

He came inside her with a feeling of triumph, as though he'd made a conquest that would change his life. He felt his own strength, felt her softness, and knew it was the way this was meant to be. For just a moment he was all feeling, all sensation, spinning in space, clinging to her for support, his lifeline back to earth and reality.

"Wow," she whispered when it was over and he was stroking her face. "I guess we aren't in Kansas anymore."

He smiled and dropped a kiss on her lips.

"We swore we wouldn't do it outside the bedroom again," she reminded him.

"We lied," he told her simply. "We can do it wherever we damn well please."

She laughed at that. He was right. If only he would amend that to "whenever," as well. Because, full of joy as she was at his unexpected return to claim her, she knew it was only temporary. He would go next time. And she would be left behind.

Ten

This was ridiculous. Just the week before she hadn't known him. And now she felt as though she couldn't live without him. Pathetic. The women's liberation movement better not get wind of this. They'd have her strung up by her thumbs from a clothesline.

Obviously, she was too dependent. She had to be more assertive. She had to learn to take care of herself emotionally. After all, if she was going to be unable to form a decent relationship with a man, she'd better get used to this. She was going to be alone for the rest of her life.

But she didn't want to be—she wanted Kam. She yearned for Kam. She didn't like life nearly as much without him. She was ready to walk on hot coals to have him.

"Can't live with them, can't live without them." She was beginning to think the latter was truer than the former. She was at a point where she was about ready to think about trying. Somehow a relationship with Kam seemed doable in a way other relationships never had.

In fact, it was true. She no longer wanted to try life without him. She was even letting that word that had horrified her only days before creep into her thinking—marriage.

The days passed pleasantly enough, despite her loneliness. She quickly developed a good working relationship with Shawnee. They had liked each other from the beginning. She found herself hanging around the restaurant even after her shift was over, helping Shawnee with management details.

In the weeks that followed, she got to know practically everyone in the Caine family. Shawnee was a sort of matriarch; everyone showed up at her place sooner or later.

Shawnee's husband Ken was the first person she met. She liked the easy sense of fun between the two of them. He was a lawyer, just like Kam, but he'd given up big-city law to open a local law office that handled small-time disputes and legal papers.

"I'll never get rich here," he told her when she questioned him. "But I don't think I'll die of a heart attack at forty-five, either."

Kam's brother Mack and his wife Taylor came in for a meal about once a week. He reminded her a lot of Kam, with his dark reserve. He and Taylor were very much in love, and the loving looks she caught passing between them brought on a sense of longing so deep it shook her to her core. She missed Kam. Damn it, she really did.

Then she met the youngest brother, Mitchell, and he was completely different, a wicked jokester who kept her laughing every minute. His wife, Britt, was sweet and quiet, and the twin babies they were adopting were a riot. Just over a year old, they got into everything. When they finally left after one busy afternoon, both Ashley and Shawnee collapsed in the backroom and shared a big slice of cheesecake, just to regain their equilibrium.

"How does she manage it?" Shawnee cried. "She's always so serene."

"Twins certainly are a handful," Ashley agreed, her fork poised.

But her mind was wandering. Babies. What wonderful things. How did one know when one was pregnant? She'd never been. She didn't know. Still, something very strange seemed to be happening to her body, and now and then she had a feeling....

No, it couldn't be. Things like that just didn't happen to her.

The days went by, and Kam didn't call. He called Shawnee a time or two, and the main thrust of his call seemed to be to check on Ashley, but he never called her directly. Shawnee tried to pin him down on why he was being so cruel, but he evaded answering.

"He's scared of you," Shawnee guessed when Ashley brought it up. "That's got to be it."

Ashley laughed. The concept was absurd. "Why on earth would your brother be scared of me?"

Shawnee considered before answering. "You know that for years I've had a project. I've been trying to get Kam married. At times it's been my major goal in life."

"To get your brother married?" Ashley very carefully looked at her fingernails. "But, what if he doesn't want to get married?"

"Ha! That's exactly the situation. He doesn't want to get married." She pursed her lips. "A few years ago, before I was married myself, I might have had some sympathy for that. But now I know there's nothing like it. And I won't stop until I've got Kam married, too."

Ashley tended to shy away from that kind of determination. She didn't want to become part of one of Shawnee's projects. At the same time, she couldn't help but wish there was something she could do to show Kam he didn't have to be afraid that she would try to trap him into anything.

She had no intention of doing any such thing. If he didn't want anything as permanent as marriage, she could probably live with that. But she wanted to be with him, and she was hurt and bewildered that he seemed to be able to do without her. If he would only call, if he would only explain.

She seemed to be drifting, waiting, as though in the eye of the storm. Something was going to happen, but she didn't know what it was. And in the meantime, she would wait. And wait.

"For years, as I told you yesterday, I've been trying to find the right girl for Kam," Shawnee mentioned the next day as they were clearing up a cash register imbalance. "But now I've given up."

"Lost cause, huh?" Ashley noted dryly.

"No." Shawnee's gaze flickered over her. "I think he's found the right girl at last."

"Oh?" Ashley said, carefully avoiding her gaze as she counted out one dollar bills. "Who?"

"You."

"Me?" she shook her head, laughing ruefully. "I don't think so."

"Why not?"

She sighed, laying down the pack of money. "I'm no good at relationships. The inability to commit runs in my family. Everything I've tried along those lines has failed. A lasting relationship just isn't in the cards for me."

Actually, she was overstating her case, spouting wisdom from days gone by, things she no longer believed. She'd mulled over what Kam had said—how she didn't have to follow in her parents' footsteps— and she tended to think he might be right. The trouble was, Kam was the only one she would ever want to test that theory on, but Kam wasn't available. So it might be best to stick to the old story and not get people's hopes up.

"Don't be ridiculous," Shawnee was saying. "You're no good at *bad* relationships, but this will be a good one, and you'll be great at it. You just wait and see."

Shawnee was a bit more optimistic than she was. Ashley would wait, all right. That seemed to be her pastime these days. There was no question that she worked hard at the café. But in the evenings, with no new project from her publisher, she spent most of her time thinking about what she was going to do, about Kam and what he was doing in Honolulu, and wondering why he hadn't called. She seemed to have so much time to think lately, she sometimes felt as though she couldn't keep a thought in her head long enough to deal with it. Why did her thoughts seem so off-the-wall lately? Why didn't Kam call? And why was she so hungry in the morning?

"I have to make the bank deposits and spend some time on the accounts today. Would you be good enough to take Cousin Reggie his lunch?" Shawnee asked as she tucked the packet of money into a little green bag.

Grabbing her keys from under the counter, Ashley thought about Kam's uncle and his forlorn vigil at sea. Though she had heard a lot about him since starting at the café, she had yet to meet this eccentric member of the family.

"No problem. I'll drop it off on my way home, if you'll tell me where to find him."

"He lives in a little lean-to he'd put together on the cliffs overlooking the bay.... Just like a homeless person," Shawnee lamented. "It makes us look bad, like we don't really care about him. And anyway, he has a perfectly good apartment in town. But he has to go out there and wait for his mermaid."

"How did he ever get the idea that a mermaid was to come to him there?"

Shawnee sighed. "It all started a long time ago when he got an advance to film a special documentary on the mermaids of Hamakua Point."

Ashley was impressed. "Oh, how neat. There were really mermaids there?"

Shawnee rolled her eyes and grimaced. "No. Of course not."

Ashley was puzzled by that. "Then why....?"

Shawnee held up a hand. "Don't ask. It's too hard to explain."

"Shawnee," Ashley said softly, "have you thought about getting him psychiatric help?"

"Thought about it? I've had doctors out there to talk to him. Each and every one has come back telling me he's as sane as I am. Can you believe it? I'll tell you what I think. I think *they're* the ones who need therapy."

Ashley felt a little trepidation taking the hamburgers to this strange man, but he soon put her at ease. He was tall and handsome, with silver at his temples, and he managed to look well-groomed despite his rough living accommodations. "Come on in," he told her, opening his tiny shack to her.

She went in hesitantly, but it was neat and clean and the walls were covered with charcoal drawings of mermaids.

"These are lovely," she said, going from one to another. "Who did these?"

They were crudely drawn but there was something appealing about them. They reminded her of the American Primitive style.

"I love them," she said, once Reggie had claimed them as his own. "You should think about doing picture book illustrating. You have a very unique style."

"I only do mermaids," he told her serenely. "Only mermaids."

"Oh." She didn't know how to respond to that.

"Well," he said abruptly. "I've got to get back to work."

"What is your work?" Ashley asked brightly.

"Watching the horizon," he said, holding up his binoculars as though she were a half-wit. "What did you think?"

"As you can see, there is the suspicion of a weak link somewhere in our genetic makeup," Shawnee grumbled the next morning when Ashley told her about her visit. "I can't tell you how awful it is when people ask, 'Whatever happened to Reggie?' He used to be a cool guy, honest."

"He was the greatest." Shawnee's son Jimmy, who had dropped in to the café, chimed in. "I worked on that documentary with him and he wasn't like that then.''

Shawnee shook her head.

"Don't worry." Jimmy grinned at his mother. A tall, engaging young man, he looked a lot like his uncles. "Reggie always comes back from his bouts of lunacy. He'll come back from this one, too."

"I don't know," Shawnee said, shaking her head sadly.

But she quickly lost the melancholy as she and Jimmy sat down to discuss his upcoming trip to the Far East.

"He's taking a year off school," she explained to Ashley when she came to their table to refill their coffee mugs. "He's getting over a breakup with his girlfriend and he needs a change of scene. And since he's paying for half of it himself, I'm loaning him the rest, and his father is giving him a present, too, to make sure he has plenty of spending money. He's taking the train through Japan and backpacking all over South East Asia and spending time in Australia. It will be a wonderful experience."

Of course it would, but later, as she heard Shawnee sniffle as she waved to Jimmy from the café window, Ashley knew that it was also going to be hard for Shawnee to lose her son for twelve months. It was always hard having to say goodbye to loved ones. She'd never realized how hard until lately—and it had only been one month since Kam had returned to Honolulu.

"Why isn't he coming back?" she cried at last to Shawnee as she joined her at the window. "It's been over a month now. Why hasn't Kam come back for at least a weekend?"

"What do you mean? He never comes back that often." But Shawnee couldn't look her in the eye.

"Why couldn't he have come back at least once to see me?" Ashley asked softly, staring out into the green jungle across the road from the café.

"You got me." Shawnee frowned. "It may be time we did something about it."

She called him the very next night. "Why are you still in Honolulu?" she demanded the moment he answered the phone.

"I've got a job here, remember?"

"Don't you care about Ashley?"

There was a long silence on the other end. "Of course, I care about Ashley," he admitted at last. "But she can take care of herself, can't she?"

"Maybe."

His voice sharpened. "What do you mean? What's wrong?"

"Nothing. Except that she misses you."

He sighed. "Shawnee, just stay out of it, okay?"

"You don't want to fall in love again. Is that it?"

"It's none of your business."

Shawnee gripped the phone as though it were a bat. "You know what I think? I think you're hiding in the neat, tidy world of the law, where everything is logical and you don't have to deal with feelings."

There was silence, and when he spoke again, there was an edge of annoyance to his voice.

"I'll come back when I can. Now go to bed and get some sleep so you won't have these illusions that you can help people run their lives."

Shawnee's words stayed with him long after he'd hung up the phone. Of course he cared about Ashley. What did she think? He cared about Ashley so much, he didn't dare go back and see her too soon. He was hoping the feeling would fade. But so far, he hadn't had any luck on that score.

She was in his mind day and night. He missed her so badly, there were times he couldn't sleep. How could you miss someone like that, when you barely knew them? Was he missing reality, or some sort of dream he'd concocted in his head?

He tried to convince himself that that was the case, but it wouldn't fly. He missed the flesh-and-blood woman he'd held in his arms, missed her so much he ached for her.

At first, he'd thought she was a lot like Ellen, but the better he'd gotten to know Ashley, the more he knew that wasn't true. Ellen had been wild and willful. She'd grabbed at danger, lived for the thrill.

Ashley wasn't that way at all. She tended to be impulsive, carefree, and ended up getting involved in some risky activities now and then. But the purpose of her life wasn't risk—the way it had been for Ellen.

He now realized that Ashley could probably handle herself quite nicely. She didn't need a keeper. He didn't have to worry that she would do something stupid every time he let up his guard, the way he had with Ellen.

So why couldn't he let himself love her? What was the matter with him? He didn't know what it was for sure. He just knew that it scared him too much.

"More time," he told himself softly. "I just need more time. Then I'll know for sure."

Ashley's parents came to see her before leaving for the mainland. To her surprise, they arrived together and there was no sign of Eric or Christina. It soon became apparent that they were a twosome again, a situation that first bewildered, then infuriated Ashley.

"Isn't it wonderful?" her mother crowed, showing off a new diamond. "We're going to get remarried."

Ashley's face was set stubbornly. She crossed her arms over her chest and stood her ground. "No," she ordered firmly. "I won't allow it."

They gaped at her.

"But . . . b-but . . ." was all her father could get out.

"Ashley, darling, this should be just what you've always wanted," her mother chimed in, baffled.

Ashley shook her head. "No deal," she told them both sternly.

"But, Ashley," her father pleaded. "We love each other. Won't you give us your blessing?"

She relented only slightly. "Here's what we'll do. I want a six-month waiting period. Those are my conditions. You two have been going through your lives making reckless choices that hurt other people. For once I want you to plan something out. Try to keep a commitment for six months. And if you do, and you still want to get remarried, I'll give you the biggest wedding this side of British royalty."

They reacted like chastised children, defensive at first, weepy at the end. But they agreed to her terms.

"Six months," her mother reminded her as they left the beach house. "We'll be back. And then we'll honeymoon in Hawaii."

Ashley had her doubts. Six months was an awfully long time for the two of them to stay in love. She had her hopes, but she'd had too many disappointments through her life with those two to count on anything.

"I'm not like them," she reminded herself, sitting beneath a palm tree and staring into the ocean in a melancholy mood. And then she carefully put her hands over her stomach, wondering. . . .

* * *

"It's the sensation of the season," Shawnee announced the next morning. "Reggie has caught his mermaid."

"What are you talking about?" Ashley demanded.

"I'm talking about mermaids. I'm talking about fantasies coming true. I'm talking about a world that's gone a little too crazy for me."

"Okay, take it from the top. What, exactly, has happened?"

Shawnee took a deep breath and leaned against the counter. After a quick glance out at her clientele to make sure everyone was cared for, she began.

"He's got her. He's in heaven. It's all so insane. It seems he came out early this morning, just at dawn, and there was something strange moving toward the rocks. He says he knew right away it was her. He could feel it, he says." Shawnee shrugged. "And after all this, I'm not going to doubt him."

Ashley frowned, still confused. "But what was it?"

"A woman. She'd been out sailing or something and the boat had capsized. She'd been clinging to a piece of wood all night."

"So she wasn't really a mermaid." It was rather disappointing, but logic dictated it be true.

Shawnee laughed shortly. "Try telling Reggie that." She threw up her hands. "All I know—all I can tell you—is what the doctor said. If he hadn't been there watching for her, if he hadn't pulled her out of those rocks, she would be dead right now."

Ashley narrowed her eyes, looking into a world beyond the one they inhabited. "She owes her life to him," she said softly. "How wonderful."

"What I don't get is this," Shawnee said softly, leaning close and speaking in conspiratorial tones.

"He's been waiting there for months for her to show up. And she did. Now how did he know?"

Ashley stared at her and slowly shook her head. "He didn't know. He couldn't have known. It was just a coincidence that she landed on his shore."

"Maybe. Maybe not." Shawnee shook her head, her eyebrows raised. "But he waited. And now she's come."

They were both quiet for a moment.

"Does he think he's in love with her?" Ashley asked.

"Sure. And she seems ready to reciprocate."

"Well, naturally. She was half drowned and he saved her. She's grateful."

Shawnee shook her head. "The doctor said it was more than that. Something almost spiritual, he said. As though they'd known each other in another life."

Ashley bit her lip, frowning thoughtfully. "That's crazy," she said softly.

"Uh-huh," Shawnee agreed. "Reggie's always been a little crazy. Maybe his mermaid has been, too."

"But then...what's it all about?" Ashley asked, staring at her friend.

"You got me."

They leaned together quietly for another few moments, pondering the strange quirks of fate, then they shrugged and went on with their day.

But the lesson was learned. Reggie had waited, and he had eventually gained his objective. Did that always happen? Or was it just a bit of luck?

Hard to say. Meanwhile, Ashley waited, and she was beginning to think she was waiting in vain.

Waiting. That was all she did—wait and wait and wait. Kam never came home. He promised often enough, but something always happened. The weekend before Halloween, he had a case held over and he had to stay to work on it. The second weekend in November, his client tried to commit suicide and he felt he had to stay to help him get through his recovery. The next weekend, he had a cold and stayed home in bed.

"These excuses are getting more and more transparent," Ashley fumed to Shawnee. "He doesn't want to come, because he doesn't want to see me."

"No, that can't be it."

"It is it. Believe me."

"He always asks about you. He seems so worried you might be doing something risky or dangerous."

Ashley nodded. "That goes back to the tragedy with Ellen," she said softly.

Shawnee hesitated. "Yes, probably. But what I mean is, he obviously cares."

Ashley turned and looked at her with haunted eyes. "If he really cared, he'd be here. That's all there is to it."

Shawnee sighed because she knew Ashley was right. "So what are we going to do about it?" she said at last.

Ashley shook her head. "I'm about to give up," she said, feeling forlorn. "I can't force the man to want me. I think I'd better start making plans to go home to San Diego."

Shawnee protested feebly, but her heart wasn't in it. If Kam was determined to be such a jerk, what could she do?

Ashley was at Shawnee's when Kam called the next day. He had another excuse. His apartment had been flooded. He had to stay and supervise the mop-up.

Ashley sat on Shawnee's couch, feeling suddenly sick to her stomach. He was never coming. That much was clear. She was going to leave Hawaii and never see him again. And she couldn't stand to think that.

An idea occurred to her. She turned her head slowly, giving Shawnee a sly look.

"Tell him I'm going hang gliding," she said quietly.

Shawnee placed her hand over the receiver and looked askance. "What? You're not doing any such thing."

"Of course not," Ashley said serenely. "Just tell him." She stretched her legs out in front of her and narrowed her eyes. "Tell him, if he doesn't show up here tomorrow, I'll be hang gliding from the tallest cliff I can find."

Shawnee frowned, not sure this was the way to go, but she did as Ashley asked. When she hung up the telephone, she did so very slowly.

"What did he say?" Ashley asked, searching her face for clues.

"Nothing," she said, looking at Ashley curiously. "He just swore and hung up."

Great. Butterflies trembled in her stomach. Either he was so angry with her he wanted to wash his hands of the whole situation—or he was calling the airlines to book the next flight over. She should know pretty soon, either way. All she could do was wait. Again.

Kam was on his way to the airport. He was going to see Ashley, even though the prospect scared him to death.

Hang gliding. There was no way he was going to let her do that. Was she crazy?

As he boarded the plane, his mind went over what he'd seen her do—run from a wedding, challenge the town to pool, take on her parents, confront Wesley. And force Kam himself to take a fresh look at his life and his needs.

Yes, she was perfectly capable of trying hang gliding.

"Over my dead body," he muttered. The person seated next to him looked alarmed.

He was such an idiot. Why had it taken him so long to face the fact that he needed Ashley in his life? That he'd been kidding himself all along, that he needed someone, and wasn't some sort of archetypal loner who could stand against the wind.

He was finally coming to terms with the fact that he'd been hiding from the truth all these years. It wasn't Ellen's death that had destroyed his ability to contemplate joining his life with that of another woman. It was women themselves. Shawnee was right. He'd been hiding in the formal structure of the law, taking comfort in its rules and regulations, so that he wouldn't have to face the complex mystery that made women what they were.

He'd always liked women. But they'd mystified him, and he didn't like it when things did that. He didn't know why women did the things they did, thought the things they thought. When he was with a woman, he didn't know where he stood, could never predict what she was going to do next, felt as though he were stepping, blindfolded, into quicksand.

Ellen had been a pure example of that. She'd been careless and wild, always leaping off cliffs and expecting him to catch her. Just one time he'd neglected to show up for that part of it, and she'd died as a consequence. And he'd decided at the time he wasn't going to risk that again. He only wanted to be responsible for things that were actually under his control. In a word, himself. For years, he'd shied away from anything else.

But with Ashley, it had been different. She'd been so open with him, so honest about every detail of her life and what she thought, that he had less grounds for complaint. And still he had run from her.

That was over now. He was running to her. He only hoped he wasn't too late.

Ashley was getting ready for bed when he walked in the door. She came out to the living room and stared at him, not smiling.

"Hello," he said, hands in the pockets of his slacks as he gazed at her levelly. "I'm back."

"So I see," she acknowledged. He looked wonderful, but she wasn't about to let him see her real reaction. Her chin rose and she stared at him. "I take it you don't want me to go hang gliding."

He nodded slowly, his green eyes burning with emerald fire. "I not only don't want you to. I forbid it."

"Forbid." She rolled the word on her tongue. "Forbid. What a strange word." Her eyes narrowed. "And how inappropriate."

He stepped forward until he was right in front of her, looking down into her defiant face. "So, are you a roaring feminist all of a sudden?"

She shook her head, her gaze still holding his. "No, not really. But I am a person in my own right, and I don't take kindly to having someone *forbid* me to do anything."

"Well, I forbid you," he said again, his face hard and unrelenting. "And I claim that right by virtue of this."

He grabbed her. There was no other way to describe it. Reaching out, he grabbed her and pulled her into his arms, and though he was rough at first, his mouth, when it covered hers, was tender and sweet, caressing rather than punishing.

She tried to pull away. After all, he'd ignored her for weeks. What right did he have to come back here and expect her to fall at his feet?

"Let me go!" she insisted, pushing at him.

He loosened the circle of his arms, but only to give her breathing room. "I'll never let you go again," he told her, his gaze steaming as he looked at her, his body tense, starved for her.

"What?" she murmured, not sure she'd heard that right. She stopped struggling and looked into his eyes, searching for the facts behind the sound. "What did you say?"

He touched her cheek. "I love you, Ashley," he said, and his own eyes opened wide with surprise. He'd never said those words before, never even thought them, and he was as shocked as she was by how they sounded in his voice.

She laughed—laughed at his own reaction to what he'd said, laughed because she was so happy, because she wasn't sure if this were really happening or if she was having a lovely dream.

Then she hesitated. Should she tell him she loved him, too? Why not? After all, if it were only a dream, it wouldn't matter.

"I love you, Kam," she said loud and clear. "I've loved you for weeks." Her hands flattened against his chest and she felt his heart beating like a drum. This was no dream. Her heart soared. "And I'm so mad at you," she added, looking up at him, "for wasting so much time!"

His laughter joined hers, and he looked down at her in wonder. She was his, and the fear was ebbing away. Funny, but now he realized that the one thing that scared him more than loving her was losing her.

They made love in the living room again, slow, sweet love that felt like a swim in a lake of warm clouds, until the end, when it felt like a race to the moon. When he burst inside her, she felt as though the world were exploding around her. She was just a little surprised to find everything intact when she regained true consciousness.

"You are the most super lover in the world," she murmured happily, her body still curled into his.

"I guess you're telling me that out of your vast experience," he teased, biting her earlobe softly.

She giggled. "I don't need experience to know that, my love. All I need is the way I feel when you touch me."

He hesitated. There was one more hurdle to leap. Knowing how she felt about herself and relationships, he wasn't sure how she would take this.

"Ashley," he said seriously, rising to look down at her. "I know you're gun-shy about getting married."

She nodded slowly, looking at him in wonder.

"If you need more time, we can wait," he said. "But I want you to start adjusting to the inevitability of it."

She blinked. "The inevitability of what?" she asked, bewildered.

He hesitated. "Us getting married," he said very quickly, getting it all out at once.

"What?" She rose and stared at him. "You can't mean it!"

He pulled her back toward him. "I know this is hard for you to do," he told her. "But I want us bound together formally as well as emotionally. Can you understand that? I need the legal structure of it. And besides, when we have children—"

"Kids! You even want kids!" She gaped at him, unbelieving.

"You want kids, don't you? We have to have kids. If you're really opposed—"

"Opposed?" She fell over on her side, laughing and close to hysteria. "Opposed?" she cried out. "Kam, you crazy man, I think I'm already pregnant with your child."

"My God." His gaze fell to her stomach and he touched it tenderly, reverently. "Oh, my God."

She smiled, watching him, tears welling in her eyes. "I thought you would be upset," she whispered tremulously.

"Upset?" He took her in his arms and rocked her close. "Ashley, I love you," he said, and this time it sounded so natural.

"I love you, too," she muttered, sniffing. "I can't tell you how much."

He smiled, breathing in the scent of her hair. He had a new sense of purpose, and knowing himself as he did, he knew that making her happy was about to become his new obsession.

But that was as it should be. This was what he'd needed. This was a healing he'd only dreamed of. She was the other half of his whole. He would never feel that dreadful loneliness again, because forever, together or apart, he would have her in his heart.

*   *   *   *   *

♥ SILHOUETTE

Desire

COMING NEXT MONTH

AN OBSOLETE MAN Lass Small

Man of the Month

Rugged Texas cowboy Clinton Terrell was a basic man; Wallis Witherspoon should accept that she was a woman and stop being so independent and fearless! She looked like a female; why couldn't she act like one?

THE HEADSTRONG BRIDE Joan Johnston

The latest novel featuring the Whitelaw family.

Sam Longstreet planned to woo and wed Callen Whitelaw all in the name of revenge, but he hadn't planned *loving* his headstrong bride!

HOMETOWN WEDDING Pamela Macaluso

Just Married

The princess fell in love with the pauper, but she said she wouldn't marry him. He left, made his fortune and came home; would she marry him now?

MURDOCK'S FAMILY Paula Detmer Riggs

Funny how when he faced death Cairn Murdock realized what was most important in his life…a home, children, a wife. Cairn was about to break his word to his ex and walk back into his family's lives…

A LAWLESS MAN Elizabeth Bevarly

Sarah Greenleaf was driving Griffin Lawless crazy. He was an officer of the law and the way she was making him feel was downright criminal!

SEDUCED Metsy Hingle

Amanda Bennett was fond of Michael Grayson's little niece, but she'd fallen hard for him and so she wouldn't be seduced into marriage unless he proved his intentions were honourable.

SILHOUETTE

Sensation

COMING NEXT MONTH

DRAGONSLAYER Emilie Richards

He Who Dares

Thomas Stonehill had lost his faith in God and in himself, but he was doing the best he could and so was Garnet Anthony. But Garnet had made some enemies and Thomas knew he couldn't protect her unless she came to live with him. Trouble was, a preacher couldn't live in sin...

FINALLY A FATHER Marilyn Pappano

He had a daughter and he had a right to know. But it had been ten long years, once the secret was out would anyone forgive her? Would she find herself at the heart of a family...or on the outside looking in?

TWO FOR THE ROAD Mary Anne Wilson

Sister, Sister Duet

Jackson Graham had better things to do than baby–sit some mobster's mistress until she could testify and he let his beautiful witness know it. Ali didn't want to be around when he found out he had the wrong twin in his protective custody—Jack was just as dangerous as the bad guys!

SHADES OF WYOMING Ann Williams

When Julia Southern's car conked out in rural Wyoming, she didn't expect to be rescued by a suspicious cowboy right out of the wild west! After all, it was the 1990's...wasn't it? And why was Ryder McCall so suspicious and secretive?

 **SILHOUETTE**

⟩ SPECIAL EDITION ⟨

COMING NEXT MONTH

FOR THE BABY'S SAKE Christine Rimmer

That Special Woman!

Andie McCreary was an independent, self-sufficient person, and she was perfectly capable of taking care of herself and her unborn child. But Clay Barrett wanted to be her husband and the baby's father. Was it all just for the baby's sake?

C IS FOR COWBOY Lisa Jackson

Love Letters

Sloan Redhawk owed Jenner McKee big time, so when Jenner wrote and asked Sloan to find Casey McKee, who'd been abducted, Sloan couldn't say no.

ONE STEP AWAY Sherryl Woods

Ken Hutchinson was like Beth Callahan's dream come true. There was only one fly in the ointment—Ken's seven-year-old imp of a daughter was determined that her daddy remain single!

A DAD FOR BILLIE Susan Mallery

It was sweet torture watching the bond develop between Adam Barrington and her daughter Billie, thought Jane Southwick. It was pure joy to see them together despite her guilty secret.

JAKE RYKER'S BACK IN TOWN
Jennifer Mikels

Jake Ryker had come back to fight for the love he'd left behind all those years ago when he'd been a rebel on the wrong side of the law. What had happened to the girl he'd left bereft?

THAT SPECIAL SUNDAY Maggi Charles

Russell Brandon Parkhurst had lied to Paula. He'd been less than honest about his huge fortune, his rocky youth and even his name. Why should she believe he loved her?

▼ SILHOUETTE

Intrigue

COMING NEXT MONTH

FOR LOVE OR MONEY M. J. Rodgers

Detective Samantha Turner could find no motive for the
murder of heiress Joni Wilson. Scott Lawrence was helping her
in the investigation—*and* helping her to trust in love again. But
just how much *could* she trust him when he stood to gain
financially if this mysterious case was solved?

DOMINOES Laura Gordon

The first victim was her best friend. Then a woman whose name
was hauntingly familiar. Then another…And the only common
link among them was that they had known Kelsey St. James.
Kelsey was looking for help—and found it in tough cop Ben
Tanner.

LOST INNOCENCE Tina Vasilos

Alexa recalled nothing of her childhood, but when a stranger said
her father was alive, she set off for the Greek islands. Right after
her arrival, she was found sleepwalking…and a man was dead.

THE MASTER DETECTIVE Heather McCann

Margaret Webster knew her precocious niece was no angel.
Especially when she was hell-bent on proving her stepfather was
plotting a ghoulish murder. Then when Jake McCall arrived, with
his dark hair and equally dark identity, he was a living, chilling
reminder that anything was possible.

SLOW BURN
Heather Graham Pozzessere

Faced with the brutal murder of her
husband, Spencer Huntington demands
answers from the one man who should have
them—David Delgado—ex-cop, her
husband's former partner and best
friend…and her former lover.

Bound by a reluctant partnership, Spencer
and David find their loyalties tested by
desires they can't deny. Their search for the
truth takes them from the glittering world of
Miami high society to the dark and
dangerous underbelly of the city—while
around them swirl the tortured secrets and
desperate schemes of a killer driven to
commit his final act of violence.

"Suspenseful…Sensual…Captivating…"
Romantic Times (USA)

MIRA

SECRET OF THE STONE
Barbara Delinsky

Paige Mattheson was reputed to be as
beautiful as her alabaster sculptures—and
just as cold. Her only passion was for her
work, until Jesse Dallas came along.

Her fierce desire for Jesse both exhilarated
and terrified her. They shared six glorious
weeks together at her isolated beachfront
home. But Paige knew that Jesse was a
loner and a drifter, who could walk out of
her life as easily as he'd entered it.

*"When you care enough to read the very
best, the name of Barbara Delinsky should
come immediately to mind..."*

Rave Reviews (USA)

MIRA

GET 4 BOOKS
AND A MYSTERY GIFT

Return the coupon below and we'll send you 4 Silhouette Desires and mystery gift absolutely FREE! We'll even pay the postage and packing for you.

We're making you this offer to introduce you to the benefits of Reader Service: FREE home delivery of brand-new Silhouette romances, at least a month before they are available in the shops, FREE gifts and a monthly Newsletter packed with information.

Accepting these FREE books and gift places you under no obligation to buy, you may cancel at any time, even after receiving just your free shipment. Simply complete the coupon below and send it to:

HARLEQUIN MILLS & BOON, FREEPOST, PO BOX 70, CROYDON, CR9 9EL.

- ✂ - - - - - - - - - - - -

Yes, please send me 4 free Silhouette Desires and a mystery gift. I understand that unless you hear from me, I will receive 6 superb new titles every month for just £2.20* each postage and packing free. I am under no obligation to purchase any books and I may cancel or suspend my subscription at any time, but the free books and gifts will be mine to keep in any case. (I am over 18 years of age)

NO STAMP NEEDED

1EP5SD

Ms/Mrs/Miss/Mr _____

Address _____

_____

_____ Postcode _____

mps
MAILING
PREFERENCE
SERVICE

TEARS OF THE RENEGADE
Linda Howard

The world stopped for Susan Blackstone when she saw the stranger—and her heart stopped when she learned his name. He was Cord Blackstone, the black sheep of the family, and her own cousin by marriage.

Cord had come back for just one reason: revenge. But he hadn't counted on Susan any more than she had counted on him. Searing passion became the wild card in the battle for control of the family business— and it was too soon to know who had been dealt the winning card.

"You can't just read one Linda Howard!"
Catherine Coulter

MIRA